"'Tis cold," she muttered,

but chuckled softly and hugged his arm. "But ye are warm."

"We shall not tarry long," he assured her and placed a warm hand over hers.

"Oh, sweet Goddess. Look at the moon, Desmond. Her light shimmers over the water. I have now witnessed the charm of the loch in sunlight *and* moonlight. Though our rivers are stunning on their own, they cannae rival this view. As I have told ye, our island is shrouded in mists, so ye cannae see verra far out into the sea."

Desmond's focus was not on the moon, but the beauty standing beside him. To take what he dared not possess. He marveled at her delight of the striking scene.

Ailsa turned toward him. "Thank ye, Desmond, truly."

Her nearness was overpowering, seducing him in a way he had never known. Desmond cupped her chin. Her eyes widened, and her lips parted in invitation. Moonlight and lust danced within her eyes. No longer did he battle with his mind and body, and he slowly lowered his head.

And under the silent whisper of a full moon, Desmond captured her soft lips within his own. He could taste her sweetness mixed with the wine, and desire shot through his veins. His hands shook as he placed them securely on her waist. As he deepened the kiss, she placed her hands around his neck. Desmond groaned, crushing her body against him.

Praise for Mary Morgan

"It feels so good, to discover a well-written fantastic romance filled with so much magic and passion, that you can't put it down!"

~*Books & Benches*

~*~

"The story itself is a brilliant conclusion to what has been the most fantastic journey. I am going to miss those Dragon Knights. I cannot recommend this book or this series enough. A must read."

~*Mary Yarde*

~*~

"This was my first read of Mary Morgan and I was enchanted with the world of knights, dragons, myths, magic, time-travel, love of soulmates, a druid or two, a few faes here or there, and of course a bad guy. I got a very splendidly detailed time-travel romance that would entice the soul to make that ultimate sacrifice to find that one true love that was meant to be."

~*The Book Junkie Reads*

A Highland Moon Enchantment

by

Mary Morgan

*A Spin-off from
The Order of the Dragon Knights Series*

This is a work of fiction. Names, characters, places, and incidents are either the product of the author's imagination or are used fictitiously, and any resemblance to actual persons living or dead, business establishments, events, or locales, is entirely coincidental.

A Highland Moon Enchantment

COPYRIGHT © 2017 by Mary Morgan

All rights reserved. No part of this book may be used or reproduced in any manner whatsoever without written permission of the author or The Wild Rose Press, Inc. except in the case of brief quotations embodied in critical articles or reviews.
Contact Information: info@thewildrosepress.com

Cover Art by *Debbie Taylor*

The Wild Rose Press, Inc.
PO Box 708
Adams Basin, NY 14410-0708
Visit us at www.thewildrosepress.com

Publishing History
First Fantasy Rose Edition, 2017
Print ISBN 978-1-5092-1752-6
Digital ISBN 978-1-5092-1753-3

A Spin-off from
The Order of the Dragon Knights Series
Published in the United States of America

Dedication

To Families everywhere, especially my own.
We are bonded together through blood and love.

Other books by Mary Morgan

Order of the Dragon Knights ~
Dragon Knight's Sword, Book 1
Dragon Knight's Medallion, Book 2
Dragon Knight's Axe, Book 3
Dragon Knight's Shield, Book 4
Dragon Knight's Ring, Book 5
~*~

Legends of the Fenian Warriors ~
Quest of a Warrior, Book 1
~*~

Holiday Romances ~
A Magical Highland Solstice

Prologue

When the ancient bards wove the tale of the great O'Quinlan clan in Navan, Eire, they foretold of destinies that would forever change the lives of these noble warriors.

One might deem that it all began with the eldest male, yet, the story began with the youngest—a daughter. To protect Fiona O'Quinlan from the enemy of their clan, her brother, Desmond, sought out a Fenian Fae Warrior to escort her to safety during a fierce battle.

However, as with any request to the Fae, all did not go as Desmond wished. The Fae had already set in motion their own plan, and their sister was sent to another time.

The O'Quinlan clan would not be reunited with Fiona for many years. When they were, they were told her fate was destined with another—Alastair MacKay, a feared, and battle-scarred Dragon Knight. Though Desmond and his brothers eventually accepted their sister's love for the MacKay, Desmond harbored lingering doubts over the match.

And as one year bled into the next, Desmond's anger at the MacKay grew.

Unbeknown to Desmond, his time had come to fulfill the bardic prophecy and take his place as a ruling warrior. Furthermore, in order to step forward on his

journey, he must relinquish the fury of the past and open his heart and mind to only one emotion.
Love.

Chapter One

Urquhart Castle, November 1208

"By the hounds!" Desmond bellowed, slamming a fist to Alastair's jaw. "Ye fight without honor." He glared at the Dragon Knight and pointed his sword at him.

Alastair rubbed a hand over his chin. "Are ye angry because I attacked your weak arm?"

"Nae," spat out Desmond. "'Tis not weak. Ye ken it has since healed."

"Then why the harsh words?" Alastair straightened and lifted his sword high.

"Ye dare to use *magic* to thwart my move. The ground rumbled beneath us."

Shrugging, Alastair tapped the ground with his sword. "I dinnae feel anything."

"Then ye must be getting old, Dragon Knight," taunted Desmond.

Arching a brow, Alastair lunged at him. However, Desmond reacted swiftly and moved aside, smacking the man on the back.

Stumbling slightly, Alastair turned back toward him. "Might I remind ye that ye are older by two winters?"

Desmond's mouth twitched in humor. "Aye, but ye *look* older."

"Bastard," hissed the Dragon Knight, and the battle of blades began in earnest.

For the next half-hour, the clash of blades, grunts, and curses flew out between the two men in the lists. Both were intent on drawing blood from the other. Regardless of Alastair's power over the land, Desmond continued to battle with the man. He would show no weakness in front of the Dragon Knight. Blood seeped into his eyes, causing his vision to blur, and the last blow to his jaw left him unsteady on his feet.

When his brothers arrived, followed by the other MacKays, Desmond fought harder. Leveling a fist into the man's side, he was rewarded with a kick to the knees, landing him on the ground. As Alastair readied to level his blade against his chest, Desmond rolled away and quickly stood. Wiping blood from the cut on his brow with his arm, he drew forth his dirk with his other hand.

"Two blades? Fearing for your life, O'Quinlan?" His opponent stalked him. His eyes changing colors showing the dragon beast within the MacKay.

Desmond's expression stilled and grew serious. "Should I be?"

Tension hummed around each, and a hushed silence descended for several moments.

Alastair lowered his sword. "*Never* on MacKay land."

"Agreed," shouted Angus MacKay, striding forward.

Wiping his mouth with the back of his hand, Desmond watched the oldest Dragon Knight approach him. "Good morn, Angus."

Smiling, Angus smacked a hand against his

shoulder. "Aye, 'tis a fine one to train in, but I can see there's more than an exercise of blades here between ye and Alastair."

Desmond winced from the contact, his shoulder bruised from the recent skirmish. "I can assure ye, 'tis all we came out here to do this morn." He glanced up at the sky. "And there is no fear of snow to hinder our movements."

Angus glanced over his shoulder at his youngest brother. "Truth?"

Leaning against a post, Alastair snorted. "What? Did ye think I was going to maim the O'Quinlan?"

Shaking his head, he gave Alastair a warning look. "If Fiona had witnessed the two of ye *fighting*, instead of sparring, I can assure ye she would have both your heads. Ye willnae be able to account for this once she sees your faces."

"My *wife* is my concern," protested Alastair moving away.

Desmond shrugged out of Angus's grasp. "And my *sister* will understand."

"Horse dung!" shouted Duncan MacKay from the other side of the lists.

"Agreed!" bellowed the rest of the men gathered around him.

Narrowing his eyes, Desmond pointed his sword at them. "Enough!"

Hushed silence descended as he made his way past his brothers and the other MacKays. Yet, it was Niall's words that made him halt his stride.

"Ye ken Fiona will be upset. She deems ye are still angry with Alastair for leaving her when she lay dying two years past."

He glanced sharply at his older brother. "Truly?"

Niall shook his head. "Aye. She has spoken to me. Since the moment we have returned, ye and Alastair have been sparring with words, blades, and even mead. Ye cannae even agree on the right mixture of the liquid."

Frowning, Desmond stared at Alastair's retreating form as the man departed the castle through the portcullis. "I have never stated a word to her."

Niall nudged him in the back. "Ye dinnae have to. She has seen your reaction to him. Brian—"

"Does our other brother believe this as well?" Desmond scrubbed a hand vigorously over his face.

"Aye," he uttered quietly. "Remember, ye gave a full account of what happened when ye returned home. Bitterness laced your words. I prayed the years would have lessened your anger. But I can see I was wrong."

Desmond sighed. "But I favored the union between our sister and the Dragon Knight. So let us not discuss this any further. Fiona is happy. We are *contented* with this union."

Niall moved in front of him. "Nevertheless, ye harbor a small part of anger toward the man. Ye can no longer hide behind a blade or shield. Ye must speak with Alastair."

He snarled at his brother. "The MacKay has no wish to hear my words."

Niall stepped closer. "Make amends before the Fenian Warrior comes for us tomorrow. I have no wish to leave with bitter words left unsaid and peace not attained."

Desmond gritted his teeth. Acknowledging his brother's words, he gave him a curt nod and stormed away. The bite of the wind followed him as he made his way through the portcullis and headed toward the loch. His body throbbed with the beating he took from Alastair. In truth, he longed for a hot bath to ease the pain of bruises that were still healing from a previous sparring with the Dragon Knight the other morning.

Brushing past a pine limb, he stepped into the clearing. The mists hugged the rugged edge of the hills. He watched a lone hawk making lazy circles over the trees as he tried to calm his breathing. Stripping free from his clothing, he braced his body for the icy, brittle sting of the water. Desmond would deal with the MacKay later. Now, he sought to temper the burning fire within his body and soul.

****

Fiona tapped her foot impatiently, waiting for her brothers to enter the Great Hall. She'd sent them both to make sure her brother and husband were not trying to chop off limbs from each other. Since the moment her brothers had arrived, Desmond seemed intent on provoking Alastair, and she couldn't understand his meaning. On several occasions, Fiona had witnessed Alastair's shift from man to his inner dragon, and only her touch had soothed the beast back within him.

Two years might have passed, but time apparently had not dulled whatever issue her brother had with her husband. Furthermore, Alastair seemed intent on doing his best to encourage the rage.

The Fae had granted her request two years ago to have her brothers magically escorted at this special time of the year to her new home at Urquhart Castle. She was determined to use their time together to form ties with her brothers, not only with herself, but with the

MacKays. This was their first Samhain as one family—O'Quinlan and MacKay. However, the strain of being under one roof was intolerable. Barbs were continually tossed out between her husband and brother. It was enough to have her stomach twisted into knots at the meals, fearing a fight would ensue.

Their time together was precious, so Fiona had devised a plan. One, which both men might attempt to thwart. Nonetheless, she believed it would help settle the differences between the two. She surely did not want a repeat performance on next Samhain.

Fiona leaned her head against the cool stone, trying to ease the dull pain behind her eyes. "Sweet Brigid, if they don't get in here soon, I swear I'll storm into the lists and bash both their heads together."

Hearing the doors to the castle slam open, Fiona rushed out of the Great Hall into the corridor. Her shoulders slumped when she noticed the absence of the two troublemakers. "Are they still in there?" she snapped.

Niall placed a gentle hand on her shoulder and steered her back inside the hall. "Nae. I believe both went to cool themselves by the loch."

"Did you speak with Desmond?"

He nodded. "I fear he did not take hearing my words well."

"He's as stubborn as the MacKay men," she blurted out. "Brute force seems to take precedence over talking about a problem." Seeing the other MacKay men wince at her words, she gave them a weak smile. "Sorry, but true."

Angus waved her off. "No need for amends. Ye do speak the truth." He poured some ale into a mug, handed it to her, and then began filling the other mugs for everyone as they all settled in at the table.

Fiona looked for a pitcher of water and added some into the accepted cup. Swirling the liquid, she sipped it slowly. Glancing back up, she noticed the intent gaze of Stephen MacKay. Leaving his chair, he slowly made his way to her.

He leaned near her. "Ale laced with water?"

Fiona narrowed her eyes at the man. "Angus makes the ale strong."

Smirking, he added softly, "Does Alastair ken ye are with child again?"

"Son-of-a...did Aileen tell you?"

Stephen winked. "We have nae secrets between us."

She jabbed him in the chest. "There is supposed to be a code between women. I can assume either your wife forgot, or her brain is muddled because of her *own* pregnancy," she whispered.

The man's jaw gaped open, and his eyes grew wide. "I dinnae ken," he mumbled.

Shocked by Stephen's reaction, she grabbed his hand. "Oh, no. I'm so sorry. I thought she had already told you." Fiona put her mug down and brushed a hand over her forehead. "I just assumed...gosh, I hate that word...since she's further along—"

He silenced her blabbering by placing a finger on her lips. "Dinnae fret. I should have remained silent. 'Tis my own fault for speaking thus. I shall act surprised when she tells me."

She nodded, and he led her to a seat near her brothers. Retrieving her mug, he handed it to her. Fiona took another sip to settle the queasiness inside her stomach. She prayed this pregnancy would not have the severe morning sickness she had experienced with her first child.

Placing her mug down, she clasped her hands in her lap. "Before Desmond and Alastair return, I have worked out a plan and require your help and approval."

The room became eerily quiet as each of the men stared at her.

"This tremor of unease between these men has to cease." Fiona looked to Angus. "Did you not state that the building of Aonach castle can continue until the first snowfall?"

"Aye," replied the man slowly.

"Good. Then Alastair and Desmond can head out there tomorrow. I am sure once it starts to snow, they'll be able to return safely. They can iron out their differences by working out there together. I've spoken with the other women, and they've prepared some food for their journey."

Duncan leaned back in his chair. "Do ye deem it wise to send them out—" He tapped a finger to his head in thought.

She arched a brow. "Unsupervised?"

He smiled. "Aye, that's the word ye used the other day."

"I'm tired of playing nursemaid to two grown men. I love them both fiercely and refuse to let this squabble continue."

Noticing her brothers' confused expressions, she said, "I'll explain the meaning of my words later."

"'Tis a risk ye take," stated Duncan.

"I dinnae ken your meaning, MacKay," fumed Niall, his tone low.

Fiona shifted slightly understanding Duncan's meaning and placed a calming hand on her brother's arm. "If he can't control the dragon beast, then he's no good to any of us, including me."

Duncan's eyes flashed with the brilliance of his own inner dragon, yet, he remained silent.

She glanced at Angus. The leader of the Dragon Knights often sat in quiet reflection while others around him argued. She waited patiently until he lifted his gaze to meet hers.

"'Tis a good plan. But we must all be in agreement."

Straightening herself, Fiona slowly looked at each of the men, daring them to challenge her idea.

Niall scratched behind his ear. "There is one problem I foresee."

Fiona shrugged. "There are many."

"Did ye forget the Fenian Warrior comes for us in the morn?"

Chuckling softly, she replied, "Nope. I had Stephen's wife, Aileen, send out a request to meet with the warrior earlier to discuss my idea. Ronan MacGuinness thought it was a grand plan. I'm simply asking for an additional few months for Desmond to remain here. Ronan offered to return after Midwinter to take him back to Eire."

"Then we are in agreement," pronounced Angus.

Duncan turned to Stephen. "I have spoken this before, but I deem the women have taken over Urquhart."

"We're just here for their pleasure," quipped Stephen, pouring more ale into his mug.

Angus held up his hand. "Since arrangements have

already been decided, I shall go find my wife and offer my assistance."

"Deirdre is with the horses," responded Fiona.

"Thank ye," stated Angus, giving her a smile.

"Come Duncan. Let us go search out our own women," suggested Stephen.

Fiona watched the MacKay men leave the hall and then turned to her brothers. "I know you think I should have asked you first, but I feared you would speak to Desmond about my plan."

Niall braced his arms on the table. "Nae, Fee, ye are right in forcing Desmond to make his peace with your husband. In truth, there is restlessness within his spirit. I believe there is more."

Brian snorted and drained his mug. "What he needs is to bed a woman. The man has gone without one far too long."

Fiona blinked, feeling her face heat. "Excuse me? Bedding a woman is *not* the solution. Furthermore, while we're discussing the subject of women, I think you all need to consider taking wives."

Niall let out a groan. "Fiona…"

Brian refilled his mug. "I will never be chained to one woman." He gestured outward with his hand. "When there are so many to fill my bed."

Standing, she glared at her brother. "You're pathetic! You only want sex and not the commitment. It's all the same, regardless of the century."

He slammed his mug onto the table, ale sloshing everywhere. "I dinnae like the sound of that word."

Fiona crossed her arms over her chest. "Pathetic…pitiful, sorrowful, wretched. Do you get my meaning?"

Brian stood abruptly, but Niall pulled him back down into his seat. "This is not a conversation we should be having with our beloved Fee," warned Niall.

He muttered a curse, but nodded.

Fiona blew out a frustrated breath and sat. "You're right. We should be focusing on Desmond and not the appetites of our brother."

"Ye wound me, Fee," grumbled Brian.

She gave him a small smile. "But oh, how I love you, dear brother."

He grasped her hand and placed a kiss along her knuckles. "I will miss ye."

Before she had a chance to utter a reply, Aileen came storming into the room carrying a screaming Hugh. "Problem in the playroom over toys with the other children. It seems he doesn't like to share."

Fiona stood and took her sobbing son into her arms. "What did he do now?"

Aileen fisted her hands on her hips. "While having a fit, he kicked the floor so hard the room shook."

Stroking his back, she sighed. "My wee Dragon Knight. You are so like your father."

Chapter Two

"If you listen closely, you can hear the trees whispering in the Highlands."

Gaping at his brothers in stunned silence, Desmond fought the rage to take a fist to both of them. Had they lost their minds? He placed a hand on his sword and it did not go unnoticed by Niall. "I have no wish to remain any longer at Urquhart. Do not order me like a lad."

"We all believe this to be a good idea. 'Tis only for a few months," explained Niall.

"We?" echoed Desmond and glanced at Brian. His other brother would not meet his hard stare.

"The MacKays—"

"Stop. Whose idea was it that I should remain here to assist the MacKay at Aonach?"

Niall shifted slightly. "All."

"Wrong," he countered, seeing the lie within his brother's eyes. "For I ken Alastair had no say in this plot."

"Fiona thought it best ye work out your differences with Alastair," interjected Brian.

"Ahh…and so the truth is revealed." Desmond stepped away from his brothers and fisted his hands on his hips. "Ye could have mentioned this before we came out here to meet the Fenian Warrior."

Niall placed a hand on his shoulder, and he flinched. "Mend the rift, Desmond. For *Fee*."

They were all wrong. There was no need to fix what could not be undone. They had not been here to witness their sister's pain as they made the journey back through the Great Glen several years ago. Her disposition grew sour with each passing day, snapping and cursing—angry with Alastair for leaving her in the care of his family after she had been injured in an attack. He deemed she was going to die and could not watch her passing. In addition, she filled her nights with quiet sobbing. Thank the Gods the MacKay finally came to his senses and followed them. When he offered marriage and his apologies, Desmond had let out a sigh of relief, since he was sorely tempted to bind and gag Fiona until they reached Eire.

Realizing he'd been controlled left a bitter taste within Desmond. "Safe journey," he muttered to his brothers. Retrieving his satchel, he stormed back toward the gates of Urquhart.

"At least ye get to spend Midwinter with our wee sister," shouted Brian.

He waved off their words over his shoulder, while he made his way through the portcullis. He gave no greeting when he passed Angus, Duncan, or Stephen in the bailey. Pushing open the massive doors to the castle, he dropped his satchel by the entrance to the Great Hall.

"Fiona!" he bellowed.

Brigid, Duncan's wife, wandered out from the corridor. "She's in the kitchens feeding Hugh."

Giving her a curt nod, he started forward, but she blocked his path. "Is there a problem?"

He arched a brow. "Ye ken my fury, so why ask the question?"

The woman narrowed her eyes at him. "Not exactly, so enlighten me."

Desmond's laugh was bitter. "Are all women in your time so annoying?"

Brigid snorted and linked her arm through his. "If I understand your meaning, then yes, we're demanding *or* annoying. Although, it seems women are the same in this time, too. Though here, they tend to have a more subtle approach."

Her beauty and charm soothed his anger as she tugged him along the corridor. "I dinnae ken the word," he stated, trying not to smile.

She smiled. "The women in this time have a *gentler* way of persuading the men. We—Aileen, Fiona, and Deirdre can be like charging rams with our men. It has not been easy with our medieval husbands, but we are all learning."

Desmond fought the grin forming on his face. "I cannae fathom Deirdre ever being gentle."

"Damn straight," interjected Deirdre walking up alongside him. She grabbed his other arm and gave him a wink.

"Please forgive my outburst," he responded, startled by her approach.

Deirdre smiled up at him. "No need to. It's the truth. Though, I'm trying to temper my demanding tone—one which my husband, *Angus*, keeps reminding me of daily."

As they approached the kitchens, Brigid placed a hand upon his chest. "Be gentle with Fiona. She's expecting and not feeling well."

A Highland Moon Enchantment

"I dinnae ken your meaning."

She rolled her eyes. "Fiona is carrying a child. She does not do well for the first three months. It is difficult for her to keep down any food or liquids. She also suffers from headaches."

Desmond brushed a hand down the back of his neck. "Sweet Mother Danu."

Deirdre poked him in the chest. "But don't treat her like a china doll, either."

Muttering a curse, he pushed away from the women and entered the kitchens. Thankfully, both women did not enter with him. His nephew sat at the table, happily content with his large chunk of bread. Seeing Fiona sitting in a chair by the hearth, he understood Brigid's meaning. Dark circles stained the skin under her eyes, and her face was ashen.

Aileen hovered nearby attempting to hand her a mug, but Fee kept pushing it aside.

"Please let me return to my chambers," pleaded Fiona.

"Not until you drink the tea. The peppermint and thyme will help to settle your stomach. If you want, dip a piece of the bread into the mug. But you must get some liquid inside of you. You'll become dehydrated."

"Can't stand the smell," she protested.

Stepping fully inside the kitchens, Desmond approached slowly. "Good morn, Fee."

When she glanced up at him, her eyes were wary. "Is it?"

Smiling, he knelt on one knee. "Aye, since I have found out I shall be staying until after Midwinter. The last time we feasted at the Solstice was when ye were a wisp of a lass."

Fiona studied his face. "And you don't mind going out with Alastair to Aonach?"

He took her chilled hand into his. "I will not say I am overjoyed by this decision—one which was discussed without mine or Alastair's consent, but I have agreed to remain and assist your husband."

Her eyes misted with unshed tears. Squeezing his hand, she said, "Thank you. I was afraid you'd come in here and start yelling at me. I've already had a rough morning with my husband. The news did not settle well with him."

Desmond frowned. "He should consider your condition."

"Great Goddess! Does everyone know?" She shook her head. "I haven't had a chance to tell Alastair."

Desmond cupped his sister's chin. "Two requests before I depart for Aonach."

She eyed him skeptically. "I'm afraid to ask."

"'Tis only fair, considering what ye did to us," he stated dryly.

"Point taken. Continue."

"First, ye tell your husband ye are with child before we set out. Second, ye drink the tea Aileen has kindly made for ye."

"Humph! She doesn't listen to me when I tell her to get some rest. She's also pregnant with a child."

Aileen pinched her arm. "Because I don't get the sickness with my pregnancies like you do."

Fiona rubbed her arm. "True, but that hurt."

"Yeah, right. Here, please do as your brother has ordered, or I fear he won't go."

Grumbling a curse, she took the mug. "I agree to your terms, Desmond."

"Good." Standing, he pointed a finger in warning. "As soon as ye have finished your tea, ye can find Alastair and give him the grand news. I deem it will make the journey easier for us both."

Fiona saluted him. "Will do, my captain."

"Thank you, Desmond," said Aileen as she handed the mug to Fiona.

Taking his leave, he barely made it out of the kitchens when Fiona yelled, "And mend this rift you have with Alastair."

"If I don't kill him first," he muttered softly and headed for the stables.

****

Hours later, both men prepared to make their way out of the castle and along the loch. The entire family came out to wish them well, and Desmond smiled at his sister.

Aonach was two days away, and they traveled with an extra horse carrying supplies and food. Neither had spoken as they mounted their horses. Yet, Desmond knew Fiona had kept her word and told Alastair about the babe. He had witnessed their tender parting, especially when the MacKay laid a hand where the babe grew inside Fiona's womb.

Though the day was brisk, the sun remained a warm beacon on their journey north through the Great Glen. Traveling along the loch for several hours, they veered away, climbing up the hill overlooking the water. Small animals skittered past them as they continued through brush and trees.

As dusk settled early, Alastair led them to a secluded area near a rocky incline. One filled with yew and pine trees. Dismounting, he spoke quietly to his horse and then pulled off his wrap and a leather sack.

"We shall stay the night here. I will fetch kindling for a fire."

Desmond gave him a curt nod and got off his mount. Clearing an area for the fire, he tended to the horses, securing them for the night. Upon returning, he found Alastair had started a fire. Dumping a small bag with food near the man, he sat on a nearby boulder.

The fire snapped in the cold night air, casting a glow on the MacKay's face. He studied the man, seeking a way to start a conversation.

Alastair pulled forth a jug from his own provisions. "*Uisge beatha?*"

"Aye, though I would have thought ye to bring some mead." Taking the jug, he took a sip. The liquid speared a fiery path within his body. Wiping his mouth with the back of his hand, he handed the jug back to Alastair.

The MacKay took a swig and stared into the flames. "There were those who deemed it best not to bring mead on this journey, so I brought the amber liquid and ale."

Desmond held out his hands to the fire, warming the chill from his bones. "Because we cannae agree on the right amount of honey, so they feared we would spout harsh words over the mead."

The man eyed him skeptically. "As if we have not done so already."

Drawing his cloak more firmly around his body, Desmond chuckled lightly. "I feel like a pawn in my sister's game."

Alastair took another sip. "She kens the game well, since I have taught her."

"God's blood, nae," he uttered softly.

Reaching for the food, Desmond opened the sack. Pulling out a small cloth covered bundle, he sniffed the contents. "Onion and mushroom pies? Must be for ye, since I have heard mention from Fiona they are your favorite." Tossing the item to Alastair, he pulled forth another. Removing the cloth, he groaned.

"Do ye not favor the meal?"

Desmond glared at the man. "Is there no meat? Surely there must be some dried beef or venison in the other pouches."

Alastair shrugged and continued to devour his meal.

Waving the food in front of the MacKay, he complained, "Just because ye do not eat the animals does not mean I must go without."

Alastair let out a growl. "Do not expect me to kill an animal to feed ye, O'Quinlan."

"Did I ask ye? Nae."

"Good. If ye have no wish to eat the food ye are holding, I will gladly take it from ye."

He smirked at the man. Taking a huge bite, Desmond savored the intense flavors mixed with herbs. No wonder the MacKay favored these tasty pies. Nevertheless, he would never admit it to the man glaring at him from across the flames. Licking his fingers, he pulled out two more, handing one to Alastair.

As they continued to eat in silence, passing the jug of *uisge beatha*, the night cloaked them, and Desmond found the tension easing somewhat. His thoughts returned to Niall's words. Aye, a part of him continued to struggle with his anger over Alastair's departure from his sister's bedside—one that left her bitter and sad. He should have banished it moons ago, yet, the moment he stepped onto MacKay land, old memories haunted him. Two full years did naught to dismiss injustices, and he struggled to remain civil.

He had shoved his thoughts away, determined to feast and celebrate the time with his sister, his nephew, and the MacKays. However, Alastair proved to be a force more stubborn than anyone. Each conversation proved to be exhausting. In addition, the sparring in the lists increased with furor.

And each day, Desmond's anger grew.

What did he actually want from the Dragon Knight? He found he could not answer the question without others spilling forth.

"Ye are thinking too much," stated Alastair, his words sounding more like a growl.

Desmond met the hard stare of the Dragon Knight. The beast was barely contained, or controlled by the man. Of all the MacKay brothers, Alastair fought the dragon each day. Love may have tamed the beast, but Desmond feared one day the dragon would become unleashed.

Tonight he had no wish to battle the Dragon Knight over the past. Weary and longing for home, Desmond settled down upon the ground. Leaning against the boulder, he watched the flames dance into the inky black sky and pulled the hood of his cloak over his head.

Sighing softly, he knew the day of reckoning between him and Alastair MacKay was fast approaching.

Chapter Three

"Heed the call when the mists of the Highlands calls forth your name."

The north wind slapped viciously, leaving its bitter sting across Ailsa's face. She gritted her teeth, as she held firm to the reins of her horse, urging her animal upward through the dense trees. Whispering soothing words to her mount, she made slow progress along a path that had seen better days. Rocks, broken branches, and mud littered the ground. Thunder rumbled in the distance, and the animal balked once again.

Ailsa halted. Lifting her head, she sniffed the air. The storm was heading their way. If they did not find shelter soon, she feared they would have to make do under the trees.

She patted the horse's neck. "We must keep moving forward, Elva. Aye, I ken ye dinnae like the smell of the air, but 'tis not safe here."

The animal snorted.

"I take it we are in agreement, or is it disgust ye are spouting?"

"Keep moving," shouted her father. "We waste time!"

Ailsa gave him a disapproving look, but moved ahead. If he had listened to her earlier in the morning, they would not be in these circumstances. She'd begged him to halt their journey until the storm passed. Yet, the great Bran MacDuff refused to hear her pleas, stating it was barely a light Highland shower. In all her years, her father had never believed in her gift to sense the storms. He had called her foolish. Aye, he believed in the old magic, but not in the daughter of a MacDuff. The special gift was reserved for sons and druids. Daughters were healers—their knowledge handed down from mother to daughter, as did her mother to her.

And now they were caught in the grip of an impending tempest.

"Can I help ye?" asked Muir. He moved alongside the animal.

She shook her head. "Elva will sense the other animal's stress."

Her father's guard glanced quickly at his horse. "My horse has seen worse and fears naught."

Ailsa tried hard not to roll her eyes at the man. "Aye, but the animal has remained safe within shelter at our home during fierce storms. This is the first time we have ventured to Scotland."

"Might I remind ye that we traveled the sea during one?"

"It was merely a light mist," she scoffed, stepping over a log.

"When we landed, the mist turned to rain," he countered.

Thunder roared closer this time, but Ailsa kept a firm hand on the reins. "Sweet Mother Danu, please show us shelter."

"Aye, Mother Danu," echoed Muir.

The path narrowed, and Ailsa waved the guard on ahead. Within moments, lightning split the gray sky, and it took all of her control to keep a steady hand on Elva's reins. Glancing over her shoulder, she scanned the area. Their druid was nowhere to be seen.

When the first drop of rain landed on her head, she swore softly. "I need ye to be strong, Elva." Leading her horse to level ground, she secured her and went in search of the druid.

Searching the trees, she yelled, "Tam! Where are ye?"

Her father would be furious if anything happened to the druid. He had specifically ordered her to watch over and protect the man.

"Tam!" Her voice was lost in the sound of more thunder as the sky opened up completely. Wiping her eyes, she crept carefully down the muddy path. A frightened bird flew out from the trees, almost colliding with her. "Bloody bastard!"

The icy rain bit into her face and hair, but she kept on moving. "Tam, if ye dinnae show yourself, I swear by all the Gods and Goddesses, I will kill ye myself."

A gust of wind made her steps unsteady. "Sweet Goddess, if ye are gathering herbs, Tam…"

Ailsa stumbled forward, grasping a hold of one of the pine trees. Searching the deep area of the forest, she breathed a sigh of relief when she saw the druid kneeling on the ground. Scratching her nose, she started toward him.

"Are ye ill?" she asked, looking around for his horse.

He remained kneeling and made no attempt to answer her.

"For the love of Mother Danu, what is wrong?" Ailsa demanded, fighting the urge to yank the man up by his robe.

Tam lifted his head and stood slowly. "Praying to the God of the storms."

"Then I pray he has listened, but we need to venture out of its path," shouted Ailsa, noticing his horse sheltered safely nearby.

Ailsa coaxed the animal with soothing words out from his shelter. Handing the reins to Tam, she motioned him forward.

"I have never seen anything so fierce," he stated over his shoulder to her.

"'Tis why we must find protection until it passes."

Making their way up the path, Ailsa greeted her own horse. Taking the reins, she followed the druid. If he reckoned it best to pray, he could do so walking. She did not want to suffer a tongue-lashing from her father again.

As the rain continued to thrash down upon them, the ground became a pool of mud, making the ascent even more difficult and dangerous. Ailsa silently cursed her father again. Her horse whinnied, sensing Ailsa's fury. Patting its thick white mane, she tried to calm the animal and her own stress.

Slipping on a slick boulder, she wiped the rain from her eyes. Glancing up, Ailsa almost shouted for joy when they came to level ground.

Muir started toward her and grabbed the reins of her horse. "Blair has found a cave. 'Tis small, so the horses must remain nearby. Ye can find it beyond the trees on the right."

Ailsa shook her head. "Nae. If lightning splinters the sky, they will panic. I will stay with them."

"'Tis madness and your father willnae allow ye to

A Highland Moon Enchantment

remain with the horses."

She shrugged. "Not his decision."

Muir let out a curse. "Follow me."

Ailsa took the reins of Tam's horse. Pointing to the trees, she ordered, "There is a cave. Go seek shelter."

Tam nodded and quickly disappeared through the pines.

Lightning seared the sky so close to them her skin prickled. They managed to escort the horses to where the rest of the animals had been secured. The enclosure was not as bad as she had expected. All the horses were safely against the rocky hill under some trees. Safe, but not enough to convince her to leave them unprotected. If they lost their horses, their journey would come to an abrupt end, leaving them without a way back to their home.

Muir gave her a disapproving look before leaving her.

"Ye may fear to cross the great MacDuff, but I have nae fear of my father," she muttered, watching him depart.

Ailsa took in her surroundings. Sitting on the cold, muddy ground was not a choice. Moving through the trees, she spotted a log partially sheltered from the elements. Saying a silent prayer of thanks, she gave one final pat to her horse and then took a seat on the log. Heaving a weary sigh, she had no sooner pulled the hood of her cloak over her head than her father's bellow echoed through the trees.

Not bothering to stand before the gruff man, she waited until he approached.

"By the hounds of Cuchulainn!" he roared. "I ordered everyone inside the cave and that includes ye!"

She lifted her head. "The horses are easily frightened. Someone must tend to them until the worst passes."

His eyes flashed with outrage. "How dare ye counter my orders!"

Ailsa stood. "And what happens if the horses trample each other. Or worse, become free and tumble down the muddy hill?"

"We can find them come morn," he barked out.

"Ye ken it is best someone stays with them, Father," she argued, trying to keep her voice calm.

He lowered his head to mere inches from her face, but Ailsa did not flinch. "'Tis my concern, *not* yours. Furthermore, I have ordered Muir to watch over them."

This time, Ailsa blinked. *So ye punish your own guard because he did not bring me back to the cave.* She started to say something, but he held up his hand in warning.

Pushing past him, she almost collided with the guard. Pausing, she leaned up to him. "There's some honeyed bread and dried beef in my pouch on Elva. Ye are welcomed to some."

He gave her a small smile. "I thank ye kindly, but I have some food."

Nodding, Ailsa made her way to and then inside the cave. The smells of men and damp earth assaulted her. A small fire blazed in the center, but it did little to banish the chill within the place. She gave a weak smile to the three guards, Gordon, Michael, and Blair, as she made her way to sit with Tam by the fire.

Holding out her hands toward the flames, Ailsa tried to warm them.

"Ye should remove your cloak," whispered Tam,

nudging her slightly.

She looked at him sideways. "It will not dry fully."

"Ye can put it on my staff."

Sighing, she complied and handed her cloak to Tam. The druid placed it over the staff and leaned it against the stone wall.

Squeezing her hands together, she huddled closer to the flames as thunder continued to roll loudly above them. "Thank ye. Where are the other guards?"

"They are gathering more wood for the fire. Dinnae fear, the storm shall soon pass," he reassured.

Ailsa closed her eyes. "Nae, Tam, the storm is a giant and will continue to lash out at the land until morn."

He leaned near her. "Ye have witnessed its power?"

Weariness settled within her bones. "Aye," she whispered and then added, "Tell my father, since he will not believe me."

"Lady Ailsa—"

Snapping her eyes open, she glared at the druid. "Please do not argue with me. Ye ken how my father would respond if I told him. I have no wish to anger him further."

His lips thinned. "He should not treat ye thus."

"Regardless, please speak with him. He will listen to your counsel." She gave him a weak smile.

"As soon as he fills his stomach, I will speak with him. He is more amiable after a meal and drink. Let me go fetch ye some food."

Chuckling softly, Ailsa nodded. *Wise plan, druid.* Pinching the bridge of her nose, she tried to fight the headache seeping in between her eyes. Lack of food and sleep did not bode well with her, especially with the arrival of the storm. She'd sensed the prickle of its power late last evening and immediately spoke with her father. Nevertheless, he would not hear her account.

If only her mother were still alive. She would have urged him to listen as she always had in the past. In truth, he never paid attention, but his mood would soften when her mother pleaded with him. However, her death brought deep anguish to him. Bran MacDuff was a force to be reckoned with when angered. Yet, now with her mother gone, he was uncontrollable. Even his own men dared not cross him at such times.

Ailsa watched the flames snap and hiss, recalling her mother's final words to her.

"Dearest, ye must convince your father to take my ashes to the Great Glen in Scotland and scatter them in the loch where the Great Dragon resides. 'Tis my last request."

"Do not speak to me of your passing. Ye will survive this sickness. Tam is making ready to leave the island and seek out other druids who ken the skill of healing."

Her mother reached for her hand, her fingers like ice as they dug into Ailsa. "Nae, I ken the time draws near."

"Ye must fight," ordered Ailsa, swallowing the lump of sadness within her throat. "We are warrior women on this island. We dinnae surrender."

"'Tis my time, dearest. I have seen the Guardian." Her mother turned her head to the light streaming in through the arched window. "She waits for me."

"Ye are too young. I will not let her take ye. Besides, Father would not wish to see ye in a strange

land."

"My people were the first keepers and protectors of the Fae dragons. We have all made the journey to where the last one resides. And ye must take me soon after my passing. Dinnae wait until spring."

"Ye are a MacDuff, and I willnae have ye spouting madness about dying," protested Bran as he entered the chamber. *"The druid will find the herbs to help heal ye."*

"Ahh...but I was an O'Neill first, my love."

Ailsa removed herself from the bedside and watched as her father sat next to her mother. He clasped her hands within his own. *"Why are ye speaking about death, Aine? Can ye not fight like our daughter asked? Ye are a warrior."*

Tears rolled down her mother's cheek. *"We all are born, and we all shall die. This is—"* Great coughing spasms wracked her frail body.

Ailsa reached for the damp cloth and handed it to her father. Watching as he wiped the blood away from her mother's mouth, she realized her mother's time was indeed slipping away. And the tears she had held back, now fell freely down her face.

Aine fought to breathe. *"Grant me this one...la...last request?"* Her eyes grew wide, pleading with the man beside her.

Bran shook his head. *"Ye ken I could never resist anything ye ask, my leannan."*

Ailsa cupped a hand over her mouth to stifle the sobs and ran out of the chamber. Her father sought her out within the hour to give her the news of her mother's passing.

"Here, eat some bread and cheese," suggested

Tam, nudging her on the shoulder, and taking a seat beside her. "I have brought ye a cup of ale, as well."

Shoving the painful memory away, Ailsa took the offered items. As she ate in silence, the food and drink did naught to banish the uneasy feeling the storm was a harbinger of something more fierce waiting for them in the Highlands.

Chapter Four

"Make a wish on the shimmer of the first Solstice star the first evening of December, and then when it fades after the full moon."

Desmond stomped his feet to ward off the chill within his body as he stood in the partial enclosure of Aonach's entrance. Rubbing his hands together, he gazed outward at the cold, frigid morning. The storm had lasted two days and brought freezing air. What fools they had been to think they could get any work done on the castle. Aye, they did manage to finish a section of the kitchens and Great Hall, but nothing more could be done.

Ten full days alone with the Dragon Knight had done naught to improve their kinship. Neither spoke much as they worked. When the sun left the sky, each was content to eat in silence and then seek his bed by the fire.

When the storm came, their moods worsened. Alastair took to his carving of chess pieces, which he favored. However, Desmond had no desire to sit still. He wandered the castle's interior, testing places that were weak or required more stone. His suggestions were received with a nod or grunt when he gave his account to the Dragon Knight.

By the Gods how Desmond longed to return to

Eire.

"Ice has taken hold of the land," commented Alastair, handing him a cup of ale.

"Aye," grumbled Desmond.

"Possibly when the sun warms the land, we can make our way back to Urquhart."

"Agreed." He took a sip of the ale and leaned against the stone. Curious, he asked, "Why did ye choose to build a new castle? I thought the Dragon Knights favored Urquhart."

Alastair swirled the contents of his cup. "A request from our sister, Meggie, when we saw her last Samhain."

Desmond had heard the tale from Fiona. All the Dragon Knights and their families traveled the veil of time into the future—one where their sister lived unbeknownst to them. There, they fought the final battle with the evil druid, Lachlan. However, their victory was overshadowed by finding out Meggie could not venture back in time with them. Her life was now in the future. They would never be able to see her again. A great loss, stated Fiona. Though she lived, the brothers still mourned her.

"Did she state why?" he asked, studying the Dragon Knight's features.

Alastair drank deeply and then wiped his mouth with the back of his hand. "Nae. She asked us to *trust* her."

"Trust," he muttered. "I ken it well with Fiona."

"Do ye?"

Desmond's hand tightened around the mug. "Aye. She continually uses the word."

"Why? Is there something amiss between ye and

her?"

He glanced sharply at Alastair. "Nae. Should there be?"

The Dragon Knight's expression hardened. "Ye speak in riddles. No better than a druid."

Desmond clenched his jaw so tightly he feared it would snap. He had no wish to discuss his relationship with Fiona, or anything else. All he wanted was to leave this place. He glanced outward at the bleak morning. "When can we depart?"

"Ye are an ass, O'Quinlan. Nevertheless, for the sake of my *wife*, I will not ask ye any more questions. We can leave in a few hours."

Fury burst inside him, and Desmond pitched the cup out into the trees. He turned on the Dragon Knight. "I am not the one who left Fiona!"

Alastair's eyes shifted, and the ground rumbled beneath them. "Explain your meaning, O'Quinlan, or I will rip it from your tongue."

"Not once, did ye make amends for leaving her! Ye did not witness her anguish and torment." He pounded his fist against his chest unable to stop the flow of words. "Ye did not travel with her and suffer her pain and fury. Thank the Gods, I did not take a blade to ye when ye first appeared on the road to find her."

Without warning, Alastair leveled a fist to Desmond's jaw. He stumbled backward, landing against the wall.

"Ye are a bastard," he spat out. "I live each day with what I did to Fiona. I was a broken man, and she healed me—soothed the dragon beast within me. It will take a *lifetime* to make amends to my wife. But I make no apologies to ye. This is between me and Fiona, not ye!" He waved his hand outward. "Is this your burning rage that has settled around ye? From the moment ye came to our door, ye have wanted to take a fist to me. Was not the blood drawn in the lists enough?" Alastair stalked toward him.

"Ye are not *worthy* of her love," snarled Desmond.

Alastair halted. A look of sadness passed over his features, and Desmond regretted the barb.

Alastair sighed. "Ye are correct. Nevertheless, I love Fiona with my verra soul. She is my *life*—the verra part of what is good. What do ye ken of the word? Have ye loved anyone where it consumed ye body and soul? Where ye made choices which were not sound? Has anyone left ye without breath and then filled ye with joy the next?"

Desmond's breathing became labored. The blow of the Dragon Knight's words slammed into him, and he looked away. "I have never loved another," he uttered quietly.

"When ye have, then we shall continue this conversation. Until then, I suggest ye mend the rift between ye and Fiona. 'Tis bad enough I have caused her pain, but I will not have anyone—no matter if they be kin, hurt her. Do ye ken my meaning, O'Quinlan?"

He glanced sharply at the man. "I would never hurt Fee."

Alastair nodded and walked away. "Prepare to depart within the hour."

Desmond's shoulders slumped. In all his life, he had never experienced what Alastair spoke about. Aye, he loved his family, but it was not the same. That kind of love was foreign to him. A word—*feeling* he could not fathom. None of the women of his village interested him. Aye, there were those who came to his bed willingly, but he had no desire to take any as a wife. Is this what was missing in his life? Was he jealous of the love the Dragon Knight and his sister had for each other?

"Nae," he growled, raking a hand through his hair. "I have nae wish to have someone cleave my heart in two. Ever."

Striding back inside, he sealed off the emotions. Soon, he would be back in Navan—*home* and life would continue as it always had—in peace.

****

Ailsa lifted her head to the warm sunshine streaming down. Stretching her arms, she worked out the stiffness in her shoulders and back. Two long days spent in the cave with her father and his guards had sapped her energy and nerves. Her father was the worst. Lashing out with harsh words, or standing by the entrance, his hands fisted on his hips. He was a man not prone to sitting for any length of time, and his foul mood affected everyone.

"Would ye care for some water?" asked Tam coming up alongside her and handing her a water skin, along with her cloak.

She almost wept for joy. "Aye, most definitely."

He chuckled softly. "I grew tired of the sour ale as well."

"I swear, when we return, I might be tempted to take over the making of the drink. Ever since my father replaced the aging Bronag with Fergus, the ale has been horrid. Bronag had a special way of making the ale. It was never bitter. When did ye have time to find fresh water?"

"There was no need, since I left the water skin open outside in the crevice of a rock during the storm."

Drinking fully, she relished the cool liquid. Handing the water skin back to the druid, she smiled at him. "Thank ye."

He shook his head. "Keep it. I have another."

"Bless ye, Tam." Tucking it against her chest, Ailsa was grateful for the simple gesture. "Is our chieftain making ready to leave?"

"Praise the Gods and Goddesses, aye."

"I will be along shortly."

"Dinnae tarry, Lady Ailsa."

She tilted her chin up. "I have no intention of stirring the ire of the great MacDuff."

"I fear we all strive to stay out of his harsh path. Furthermore, ye must remember that losing your mother was a blow to him as well."

Ailsa clenched her jaw. "Aye, as ye have stated many times on our journey."

The druid glanced up at the sky. "We all grieve differently."

She followed his movement. "There will be no more rain. Yet, I fear snow is coming."

Tam slowly lowered his head and leveled a gaze at her. "And possibly something else." He turned and made his way back to the horses.

Shaking her head, Ailsa did not have time to unravel the druid's words. Taking another sip of her precious water, she placed the water skin on the ground and proceeded to braid her hair. Finally taking the two braids, she twisted them around her head and secured the mass with one of her mother's favorite combs. One, which she wore on special occasions. Carved from the ancient rowan trees on their island, it was fashioned in the shape of a dragon with an emerald embedded in the eye. It was a cherished item, passed down from seven generations of O'Neill's.

"Ye are almost home, Mother," she whispered.

Taking a deep breath in, Ailsa released it slowly. Brushing out her gown with her hands as best she could, she adjusted the dirk on the belt around her waist. Fastening her cloak, she retrieved the water skin and made her way to her horse.

She skirted quickly to the left to avoid her father, and took the reins of her horse from Tam. Mouthing a word of thanks to the druid, she mounted and secured the water skin.

Ailsa watched as her father finally lifted his hand for all to move forward.

Although she was grateful their journey had once again begun, sadness lingered, too. They were no more than a day's ride from where they would scatter her mother's ashes. She bit the inside of her cheek when a sudden rush of emotion swept through her. The pain of saying goodbye again was too much to endure. Ailsa placed the heel of her palm against her chest.

Tam was correct. Everyone grieves differently. Perchance, she had been too harsh when it came to her father. This journey was not one he wished to take, but he did so without complaint.

All for love.

The very word was foreign to Ailsa. She bore a great love for her mother, and yes for her father also. However, she had never experienced true love for another man. Furthermore, she had no desire to marry any man from her clan. Though her parents argued she should consider the marriage offers, which were numerous, Ailsa did not see herself with any of them. Often times, she found flaws in the men—they flirted with all the other females, laughed too loudly, smelled horrid, drank excessively, and found the need to touch her in places that were not proper. In addition, a few promptly informed her that once wed, she could no longer maintain her warrior status among her clan.

Even last year, her father had threatened to marry her off without her consent. Telling her a woman of five and twenty summers was ancient, and if she did not agree to any of her suitors, then he would choose for her.

She had no wish to be in a marriage without the passion she had heard others whisper about. Ailsa had made up her mind that the man she would marry must steal the breath from her lungs, make her skin tingle with his touch, and consider her an equal when it came time for her to rule the island. Her heart yearned for love, and she would settle for nothing less.

"I could rule the island myself without any *man*," she muttered into the cold air.

Then again, she understood her people would not look favorably on a union without a husband. And a part of her longed for the touch of another—the stolen kisses she'd seen between other couples. Her mother had urged her on her deathbed to reconsider an offer soon. Time was slipping by.

Ailsa blew out a frustrated sigh. Glancing up at the sky, she realized her mother would never witness the occasion. Time had not mattered before her mother became ill. They all took it for granted. But death stole precious time away from all of them. It took her best friend, hardened her father, and sent a chilling revelation. Each day, each hour was a treasure.

Squaring her shoulders, Ailsa was now more intent on not settling for *any* man. She only prayed one day, the Gods and Goddesses would deliver him.

"Foolish thought," she snapped. "We make our own destiny. I am not going to wait for one to appear." Yet, when Ailsa glanced at her father, she understood her time of freedom without a man would soon end.

Ailsa grimaced and leaned forward to pat Elva's mane, only to hear the hiss of an arrow pass near the side of her head. Shouts erupted ahead of her, and she struggled to keep her horse steady. Instantly removing her dirk from its sheath, she watched in horror as men emerged forth from the trees.

"English," she spat out. "Go to the trees," she ordered Tam.

He departed, and she looked in horror as more of the enemy came into view.

"Get out of here!" bellowed her father as he used his shield to deflect a blow to the head.

Another arrow hurtled from the trees, taking out one of their guards. Ignoring her father's demand, Ailsa swallowed back bile and charged forward, slashing at the face of the enemy who had killed her friend. His screams tore through the air, and she kicked him hard in the side. Her foe was unprepared for her attack and fell to the ground.

"Get the woman," shouted one of their attackers.

"Ye will never take me," she snarled, as two men came charging toward her.

Turning her horse abruptly to flee, she was leveled with a blow to the back. The pain so intense, Ailsa fought the wave of dizziness. Her horse balked as her attacker tried to yank her off and onto his mount. Feigning weakness, she slumped forward. His stench clogged her senses, but she remained steady and kept her eyes on the club he had used to attack her. Leaning near the man, she lifted her dirk and shoved with all her might into his stomach. Raising her head, she gazed into eyes that held shock. Ailsa shoved him away and watched when he fell to the ground.

"You bitch. I will see you die this day!" shouted another man.

"Ye have a foul tongue—one I aim to remove from your mouth." She let her dirk fly, but the man was swifter and deflected the blade.

Glancing around, Ailsa quickly dismounted from her horse and grabbed a discarded shield and sword. Letting out a hiss from the sharp pain, she stumbled backward.

The man's laugh was sinister. "Before you die, I will take my fill of you."

Beads of sweat broke out along her brow when he dismounted. There was no time to think about her injury as his steps became predatory. She gripped the shield tighter—anticipating his first blow and praying she could hold him back. Yet, it never came. For Gordon delivered a blade to the enemy's back.

Preparing herself for the next onslaught, she fought the wave of terror when she witnessed her father battling two men. There were too many. If captured, Ailsa would suffer at the hands of the enemy. And her father would surely die trying to save her.

She watched Gordon remove his dirk from the dead man. His eyes blazed with fury. "Find shelter!"

Letting out a curse, Ailsa went to retrieve her dirk and dashed over to her horse. Grabbing the reins, she quickly got on top and took off for the dense forest. Tears stung her eyes, but she refused to let them fall. Saying a silent plea to the Gods to watch over her father and the rest of his men, she urged her horse on farther. Seeking help was her only solution. Cowering in the trees was not.

"Ye will not die, Father," she uttered on a choked sob.

Chapter Five

"Whisper your heart's desire under the stars of a Solstice eve."

Light snow fell softly into the pass and the Great Glen. Hushed silence greeted Alastair and Desmond from the forest ahead as the soft crunch of the horses' hooves echoed around them. Though the sky was gray, it was far better than the pelt of rain and wind on their backs. If the weather remained this way, then their hope was to reach Urquhart by nightfall tomorrow.

A prickling of unease slithered within Desmond.

When Alastair held his hand up in warning, Desmond swiftly placed a hand on his sword. Bringing his horse alongside the other animal, he waited. The Dragon Knight could detect more with his Fae senses. He watched Alastair pull forth his axe from the side of his horse and place it across his knees.

Lowering his head slightly, Alastair muttered, "We are being watched."

"Aye. Agreed."

"I am going to dismount."

Desmond arched a brow skeptically. "Ye deem it wise?"

His reaction seemed to amuse the Dragon Knight. "One blow to the land with my axe and it will unsettle any foe."

Squinting, Desmond tapped his chin. "True, but 'tis fear that is hiding in the shadows."

Alastair kept his gaze on the trees. "Ye think?"

"We are two men. If they wished us harm, they would have come forth."

"But the trees can make for great fighting, and any foe can attack from above." Alastair dismounted and lifted his axe over one shoulder.

Desmond looked down at the man. "Do ye reckon they are hiding among the trees?" He swiftly got off his horse and unsheathed his sword.

"Aye."

Cautiously making their way toward the pines, they halted before the forest entrance. "We ken ye are there. Come forth and make yourself known," ordered Alastair.

Silence greeted them.

Desmond stepped forward. "We wish ye nae harm."

A young man emerged from the forest, his arms held outward. "I am simply one."

"Druid?" asked Alastair.

The man's eyes grew wide. "Aye."

"Why do ye hide?"

"Because we dinnae ken if ye are foe or friend," uttered the low voice of a female behind them.

Desmond felt the blade against his back and gritted his teeth. "I can assure ye, *my lady*, we are friends. There is no need to keep a blade to my back."

"Then show me ye are a friend by dropping your weapons," she demanded.

Desmond looked to Alastair and then back to the druid. "I did not ken we had to prove our loyalty."

Dropping his sword, he lifted his hands. "Pleased?"

"Including the axe."

Alastair shrugged. "Ye may not wish me to drop my axe."

"Do not take me for a fool," she snapped.

Desmond cast a sideways glance at Alastair and understood what would happen next. The MacKay would deal with the druid, and he would take care of the woman. The Dragon Knight gave a curt nod and tossed the axe down upon the ground. The force of his power shook the area, giving Desmond the advantage he required. Dropping to the ground, he kicked the woman's legs out from under her. She toppled backward, landing on her side away from him.

Stunned, indeed, but she still maintained control of her dirk. Desmond reached for his sword and leveled it to the back of her head. "Ye are a foolish woman," he spat out. "Drop your blade and stand."

Her hand unclenched the weapon, and she turned slowly around. "Ye might as well put a blade through my heart, for I have no wish to be your captive."

Desmond stared wordlessly at the beauty before him. Eyes that mirrored the sea on a summer day gazed back at him in fury. Her hair reminded him of the wheat fields at harvest in his village of Navan, and his fingers itched to undo the mass braided around her head. Her lips thinned in disapproval, but he found himself drawn to them. As he took in her appearance, he noted the blood on her gown, and he immediately slammed the door on his lust.

Seeing his distraction, she moved her hand slowly back around the dirk.

"Nae," he uttered in a hoarse voice. "Again, leave

the weapon on the ground and stand."

She obeyed and stood slowly. Lifting her chin, she met his hard stare. "What now?"

By the hounds, he believed a warrior stood before him. However, the beauty challenging him with her words would not sway him. "Ye can give us your name and why ye put a blade to my back."

"Ye, first."

He tilted his head. "Desmond O'Quinlan, and the other man is Alastair MacKay."

"The Dragon Knight?" she uttered in a shocked tone.

"Aye," growled Alastair, keeping a firm grip on the druid's arm.

"Praise Mother Danu." The lass moved away from Desmond, and knelt on one knee in front of Alastair. "Please forgive me. We did not ken whom we could trust. My name is Ailsa MacDuff. We require your assistance."

Alastair released his hold on the druid. "Please dinnae pay homage to me." He reached down and helped her to stand.

"Ye are revered on our island," stated Ailsa. She waved her hand toward the druid. "This is Tam."

The druid nodded. "How blessed we are to have a Dragon Knight and his guard come to our aid." He looked at Ailsa. "This Dragon Knight has the power of the land."

Desmond snorted in disgust. "I am *not* his guard."

Alastair's mouth twitched in humor. "I am married to his sister."

"How can we be of service?" asked Desmond, handing Ailsa her dirk. Her name sounded familiar, yet he could not place where he had heard it mentioned.

"We were traveling to the loch when we came under attack by English soldiers. Ye must come now. Several of our guards have already been killed. My father was battling two men when he ordered me to run away."

Alastair retrieved his axe. "Bloody bastards! Our contacts have informed us King John has ordered more soldiers into these parts. We have managed to keep the peace, but this comes too close to Urquhart land."

"Then ye will help us?"

"Aye," Desmond and Alastair stated in unison.

Desmond gave a short whistle. Both of their horses trotted forward. "Did ye flee on foot?"

"Nae. Our horses are within the trees." Ailsa gave a sharp clicking sound, and a stunning white mare sauntered forth, followed by another horse.

"She is a beauty, but why would ye travel with an animal that has the color of snow?"

The lass glanced sharply at him. "*Elva* was my mother's horse. It was important she make the journey with us."

Watching as she mounted the horse, Desmond feared to ask the next question. "And your mother?"

"Dead," she replied flatly and took off through the trees.

Quickly mounting his own horse Desmond gave a curt nod to Alastair, and they proceeded to follow the lass.

Silently approaching the area where the battle took place, Ailsa dismounted and crouched down behind a large pine. Tam stayed with the horses while Alastair and Desmond both scanned the area. Evidence of the battle lay strewn everywhere. Shields, swords, and dead men scattered across the ground. Yet, the enemy was nowhere to be seen.

Ailsa started forward, and Desmond pulled her back against the tree. Her eyes blazed with fury, but he held up a finger in warning. He bent his head near her ear. "Let Alastair make sure all is secure. For all we ken, they may be hiding in the brush."

Fear reflected briefly in her features, but the lass quickly masked the emotion. Swallowing, she nodded. Releasing his hold, he watched as Alastair knelt and placed his hand upon the ground. Several moments passed before he stood and motioned them forward.

Making their way to the dead men, Ailsa ran toward an older man slumped against a boulder. Desmond was instantly at her side.

"Father," she sobbed, slumping down beside him and placing a hand near his nose. "Thank the Gods and Goddesses." She looked up at Desmond. "He lives, though his breathing is shallow."

He watched as she inspected the wound on his head and arm, noticing the odd position of the limb. "I fear 'tis broken."

"Aye," she agreed. "We must straighten the arm."

He crouched down beside her. "I can help ye. 'Tis best we do it while he is not awake."

Standing, she wiped a hand across her brow. "I will need my pouch of herbs, salves, and linens. Tam can assist me."

Desmond stood and glanced at Alastair. "Have ye found any alive?"

Alastair motioned behind him. "Only one. He took a blow to the head, but lives. Tam is tending to his injuries."

Ailsa brushed past Desmond. "Did he say who it was?"

"I believe he mentioned the name of Muir."

"Thank ye, Mother Danu," she muttered, running off in the direction Alastair gestured.

As Desmond started to follow her, Alastair blocked his movement with a hand on his shoulder. "Has the lass mentioned why they were journeying?"

"Nae."

Releasing his hold, Alastair rubbed at his face. "Why would King John's men harm travelers? I cannae fathom this senseless act of violence."

Desmond cast his gaze in the direction where the lass fled. "She did say she was a MacDuff. The MacDuff could be one of the Earls of Fife and is verra powerful. To take him down would bring a great prize. Yet, I dinnae ken if he is the one."

Alastair nodded to the injured man against the boulder. "Is he her father?"

"Aye. He lives, though has suffered a broken arm and head wound."

"Lugh's balls! 'Tis more than a day's ride to Urquhart."

Desmond frowned. "Ye would bring them into your home? What if King John finds out ye have given shelter to the MacDuff?"

"As ye ken, we have feared far worse. What is one king, when we have destroyed an evil monster intent on ridding the world of light?"

"Ye are correct."

Alastair shifted his stance. "Can ye honestly leave the lass to tend to her father and the other alone? With just a druid?"

"Nae, but—"

"By the hounds. She had ye tongue-twisted the first moment ye laid eyes on her. A few moments more, and she could have tossed her dirk into your chest," teased Alastair.

Stunned the MacKay had witnessed his momentary failing, Desmond shoved the Dragon Knight aside and made his way to where Ailsa was speaking quietly to the injured man while Tam cleaned his head wound. She kept squeezing his hand, and Desmond fought the urge to yank her from the man.

Halting his steps, he patiently waited until she was done. When she placed a kiss on his cheek, Desmond sealed off all emotion. The injured man was surely her intended.

Bending to retrieve a pouch, she turned toward him. Wiping at her eyes, she lifted her head. "Will ye assist me with my father?"

"As I have stated," replied Desmond and gestured for her to move ahead. "How many did ye lose?"

"Six good men," she answered, tucking a lock of hair around her ears.

"'Tis a blessing these two survived."

Biting her lower lip, she nodded. "My father and Muir."

Gently taking her elbow, he steered her away from the dead men. "Alastair will bury the men swiftly. With his power of the land, he can open up the ground and seal them inside. I have no wish to see ye witness this."

"Ye are most kind, but I have witnessed death many times. Furthermore, I have buried them as well. But I am grateful for the Dragon Knight's gift."

"Nevertheless, let us depart away from their bodies and leave them in peace."

She let out a frustrated sigh. "I dinnae need protection."

"And I did not offer any," countered Desmond. "I merely wished to ease your pain."

Ailsa halted and looked up at him. "'Tis all I have to hold onto. I can assure ye, I am nae damsel requiring a knight to rescue me."

Desmond stared into her eyes—ones filled with strength and sadness. He wondered if she had ever known happiness. "Have nae fear, I am not a knight, nor do I seek to rescue *any* damsels."

Mirth replaced the sadness. "Ye are a challenging man, Desmond O'Quinlan."

Not bothering to reply, Desmond turned and walked away from the woman—who in their brief encounter, left him completely bewildered.

Chapter Six

"The Snow Maiden left a trail of rose petals, praying her lover would open his heart."

Holding up her hand to stop, Ailsa jumped down from her horse.

She heard Desmond shout to Alastair to halt as she rushed ahead to her father's side. Placing a hand on his forehead, she let out a curse. His moans had only continued while they made their way toward the home of the Dragon Knight. A litter of pine boughs and branches had been lashed together for his travel. Since he continued to drift in and out, they feared he would risk falling. The wound to his head was more severe than Ailsa or Tam had thought, and they did not want to risk him riding on a horse. The journey was a demanding one as they made their way up into the Highlands.

"We must find shelter soon," complained Tam, tucking the blanket around the injured man. "Muir is faring better, but I worry about your father."

"I agree, but there is naught we can do. We must rely on the knowledge of the land from the Dragon Knight."

"'Tis fortunate he came to our aid."

"A blessing there were two men," she corrected. Snowflakes landed on her father's face, and Ailsa quickly brushed them away.

"Well, the one called Desmond is heading our way. He does not look pleased," muttered Tam.

Ailsa straighten, ignoring the shards of pain in her back. "No doubt, because I keep requesting to stop."

Turning around, she did not wait for the man to utter a complaint. "He continues to moan in his sleep. I fear if we dinnae find shelter soon, he will risk fever."

The man dared to give her a scornful look. "The delays only hinder him. I consider it wiser to let him moan as we attempt to find a place for the night."

She heard the sarcasm in his voice, and Ailsa fought to keep her hands clenched. "He is my father—our leader."

"And as a *leader*, he would agree with me."

Lifting her chin, she asked, "How much farther?"

He crossed his arms over his chest. "That would depend on how many more times ye request to halt our journey."

"None," she clipped out and made her way back to her horse.

"Good."

"Unfeeling brute. Most likely dinnae have a father." Getting back on her horse, Ailsa found him glaring at her. "What? Is there something more amiss?"

"I was nine summers when I witnessed the beheading of my father. So, aye, I did have one."

Stunned into silence by his declaration, Ailsa watched as he stormed past her. Letting out a sigh, she nudged her horse onward and recalled her mother's words from several years ago.

"Ye must learn to curb your tongue, Ailsa, when your temper strikes out."

"I wasn't angry," she argued, brushing the mane of her horse.

"True, but 'tis the same when ye are upset and dinnae have any patience. The harsh and bitter words tumble free and ye have no regrets."

Ailsa tossed the brush down. "Must Father always be so demanding? Does he not wish to see me happy?"

Her mother tossed aside one of her braids and brushed her fingers across her cheek. "Aye, but he fears that unless ye make a good match, the Isle—our home will be left to an attack by the English."

She snorted. "That's ridiculous. We are strong, and I can rule."

"Ye are wrong. The outside world will see this as an opportunity. They do not ken our ways, Ailsa. Listen to your father's counsel. He will help ye choose the right husband."

She eyed her mother skeptically. "And will ye be there to guide him as well?"

Her mother gave her a wink. "Always. For now, when the fury and distress are clawing inside ye, breathe and count to ten before ye utter one word."

"I have once again failed at the teachings ye have bestowed on me, Mother," she whispered.

Hours later when the gray light turned to night, Ailsa almost shouted for joy when Alastair led them to a shelter. Light snow continued to fall, and in doing so increased her worries over her father.

Quickly dismounting, she took in their surroundings as best she could. All she could see were trees. No cave. No place to withdraw from the elements. Brushing a hand over her brow, she made her way to her father. Dropping down next to him, she drew the hood of his cloak more firmly around him and brushed the snow from his wrap.

"Praise Mother Danu," whispered Tam and squeezed her shoulder.

"For?" she asked wearily.

"The Dragon Knight and Desmond have found a place to shelter us for the night. 'Tis not a cave, but will provide some protection."

Standing, she rubbed her hands together. "Good news. Can we make a fire?"

Before the druid could answer, Ailsa made out the embers from a blaze through the trees and smiled.

"I will wait with your father." Tam nudged her forward. "Go and take the supplies onward."

Nodding, Ailsa went back to her horse and gathered everything, including the items from her father's horse. Steadily following the light, she emerged under some branches and into a clearing near the rocky incline of a hill. In the short time, the men had cleared the area of snow, scattered pine branches onto the ground, and started a fire. Though small, it suited their needs for the night. She stood rooted to the ground, until she caught Desmond's gaze.

He pointed to his left. "We have a spot for your father in the far corner. 'Tis the best we can manage for ye and him."

Ailsa almost spouted she had survived many harsh winters outdoors in her training, but held back. Swallowing, she replied, "I thank ye."

Stepping forward, he asked, "May I assist ye with your burden?"

The light of the fire glimmered in his eyes, and Ailsa found herself staring into their green depths. Did not the hills of her home have the same color? "Aye," she whispered, answering her own question and his.

He removed the heavy satchel from her shoulder and placed it on an upturned log.

Moving slowly toward him, Ailsa dumped the remaining supplies on the branches. Wincing from the effort, she pressed a hand over her back, trying to ease the pain. Even drawing in breath was becoming difficult.

Frowning, he asked, "How severe?"

She dropped her hand. "I am fine," she lied. "Only bruising from when I was struck during the attack."

As Desmond turned to leave, she did the unthinkable and grasped his hand. The look he gave her seared a path deep inside. "Please forgive my harsh words earlier about your father. My mother often chided me for speaking thusly."

The smile came slowly. He lifted her hand and placed a kiss along her knuckles. "Ye were simply distressed over your father. I accept your amends."

"I can tend to my lady," interrupted Muir, stepping into the firelight.

Desmond immediately dropped her hand. "As it should be."

Ailsa frowned, not understanding the meaning behind Desmond's words. Watching the man depart, she fisted her hands on her hips. "I am not the one who needs tending, Muir."

"Was there a reason the man was touching ye?"

She pinched the bridge of her nose and counted slowly to ten.

"Well?"

Smiling sweetly at her friend, she replied, "I dinnae

answer to ye, Muir. Now, if ye would be so kind to allow me see to my father, since ye appear to have recovered from your own wounds."

Not giving time for the man to respond, she moved around him and quickly went to help Tam. However, once she entered the trees, Desmond and Alastair had taken charge and were bringing her father forward. Lifting the branches for them, she stepped aside. Tam followed, bringing the rest of the supplies.

As the men settled him into the sheltered place, Ailsa opened her satchel. Pulling forth herbs and salves, she focused on her task. Light spilled over her father's form, making it easy for her to inspect his head wound. There was no evidence of further swelling or bleeding. Relieved, she examined his arm. It had remained dry on the journey, and she tucked it gently under the fur wrap.

"I brought ye some warm water," uttered Tam, handing her a mug.

"Thank ye. I am not going to give him a sleeping brew. Mostly healing herbs." Tossing them in the mug, Ailsa swirled the contents.

"Aye, agreed. I will be greatly relieved once he wakes."

Ailsa snickered softly. "I'd give anything to have him issue a harsh order."

"Och, my lady." Tam sat down beside her. "Your father has a head as thick as the stones on the Isle. I have offered prayers to Mother Danu and Brigid."

She gazed down at her father. In all her life, she had never witnessed the man being so frail. His face drawn, and in the dim light, his reddish beard showed streaks of gray. When had he aged? She knew he had grieved over her mother's passing, but the man surely would never divulge his feelings to her. No, her father was more inclined to toss out barbs than to share his pain.

"Help me lift him, so I may get some of this liquid in him." Taking a cloth, Ailsa placed it under her father's chin. When she judged Tam could raise him no further, she attempted to pass some of the liquid through his lips. After several tries, they both believed they could do no more.

Tucking him back within the furs, she handed Tam the mug. "Go fetch some food and rest. I will sit with him."

"My lady, I must insist—"

"Nae. I will take first watch, and then wake ye in a couple hours."

Standing, Tam shook out his cloak. "I will bring ye some food and drink. Ale?"

Ailsa grimaced. "Mix a little with water."

Chuckling, the druid walked away.

Stretching out her legs, she winced from the pain in her back, but quickly pushed it aside. She would tend to her injury come the morning. Her father required her attention. Tam returned, bringing her some bread, dried beef, cheese, and an apple. "This is not from our supplies."

"Courtesy from the O'Quinlan," Tam explained.

Taking the offered items, she glanced over to where Desmond sat. He caught her gaze. Smiling at him, Ailsa nodded. He continued to stare at her, and she found herself drawn to his attention.

"Eat," urged Tam, settling himself nearby.

She snapped her gaze away. Yet, she knew Desmond continued to watch her from afar and heat burned her face.

Taking small bites of her food, she ate in silence. Between her meal and the watered-down ale, Ailsa started to drift. Rubbing at her eyes vigorously, she then finished her food and brushed the crumbs from her cloak. Casting her gaze to Tam, she found him snoring softly.

Checking her father one last time, she stole another look across the fire. Desmond had crouched down against a log with the hood of his cloak over his head. However, Ailsa sensed the man continued to stare at her from beneath the shadows. Call it instinct, or the prickling of her skin.

Aye, Desmond O'Quinlan. Ye are a riveting man.

Watching the embers dance into the dark night sky, she lifted her head. The beauty of the stars shimmered all around them. Angling her head, she tried to find the bear, dragon, and fox. The simple movement sent stabs of pain to her lower back. Reaching for the ale skin, she drank deeply, praying it would help ease the ache.

As the night dragged on, weariness settled into her bones. She glanced toward Tam, but didn't have the heart to wake him. Her own eyes begged to close, if only briefly. When she finally did, Ailsa sighed in relief.

****

Glorious heat invaded Ailsa's body. She floated in a peaceful place. Soothing noises flitted by her, and she tried to make out their sound. Yet, something kept tickling her nose. The more she fought to return to her dream, the more it assaulted her.

"Oh, for the love of Lugh," she muttered, coming fully awake.

Ailsa blinked in confusion before the past day's events returned with a vengeance. Glancing down, she noticed the obvious source of her displeasure and pushed the fur wrap away from her face. How long she had slept was apparent by the last star blinking down at her.

Looking to the empty spot on her left, Ailsa let out a gasp. "Father," she rasped.

Instantly, Desmond appeared by her side. "He woke during the night. With the help of Alastair, we were able to get him standing and walking about. He is faring much better."

Her eyes blurred. "Thank all the Gods and Goddesses. Do I have ye to thank for this covering?"

"Aye."

"I thank ye kindly, but now 'tis too warm."

He ignored her and placed it back over her body.

She swatted at his hand. "Leave off."

He placed a hand on her forehead. "Nae. Ye have a fever."

"Nae. Ye jest." Looking into his eyes, she smiled. "Has anyone ever told ye how beautiful the color of your eyes are?"

He gave her an incredulous look. "Never and ye are truly with fever."

Ailsa wagged a finger at him. "I have only had a fever once." She closed her eyes in recollection. "I believe the age was—"

"Five summers," stated her father, walking slowly toward her.

"Oh, Father," she sobbed out and opened her eyes. "Ye live."

The man grunted. "Of course. It will take more

than a blow to the head and broken bones to take me from this world."

Ailsa wanted to greet him. Pushing aside the fur, she turned to the side. Pain in her back slammed into her. "By the hounds, what is wrong?" she moaned, shoving a fist into her mouth to fight the wave of nausea.

"Where exactly on your back does it pain ye?" asked Desmond.

She answered his question by running a hand down her lower back.

Her father bent down beside her. "Were ye injured?"

"I believe Ailsa has suffered bruised or broken ribs," stated Desmond.

Afraid to meet her father's gaze and see disappointment, she kept her head down. "Aye. I took a blow to the middle of my back. Foolish, since I was keeping watch in front and did not anticipate the rear attack."

He cupped her chin and lifted her head. "Nae. Ye were fiercely brave, my daughter."

Her lip trembled. "I did not want to leave ye."

Pinching her cheek, the MacDuff stood. "'Tis good I did want ye to go, since ye brought back help with ye and Tam."

She gave him a weak smile. "So ye have met Desmond."

He chuckled, the laugh sounding foreign to Ailsa. "And leave it to ye to bring us a Dragon Knight, as well. Ye will take your place on the litter."

"Nae," argued Desmond. "'Tis best she remain sitting."

Giving the man a dismissive gesture, he countered, "She has a fever and most surely will fall off her horse."

"I did not plan on having her ride alone. She will ride with me."

Ailsa looked at the men battling for control of her condition. Never in her life had she witnessed any other tempt fate by arguing with her father's orders. It was a most odd scene. Desmond's face was a mask of stone, mirroring the great MacDuff.

Her father shifted his stance, holding his injured arm. "I suppose ye have knowledge of traveling with broken bones?"

"Many times," replied Desmond.

However, her father could not be swayed. He was determined to give the last order. "She will ride with my guard, Muir."

Desmond crossed his arms over his chest. "Nae. The man can barely manage his own needs. He still suffers from his head wound."

"Just strap me to my horse and tether me to another," she giggled.

Instantly, Desmond bent and scooped her into his arms. Letting out a hiss, she wrapped her arms around his neck. Glancing sideways at her father, she realized he looked as though the man had attempted to do her bodily harm.

"Let him help me, Father," she pleaded, reaching out to him.

He grasped her hand. "Before we depart, I will order Tam to make ye a brew for the fever." Turning a steely gaze to Desmond, he added, "If she worsens, I shall take your head."

Desmond actually snorted and walked away.

Ailsa studied his handsome profile. The shadow of a beard from yesterday had appeared thicker overnight, reminding her of a pirate. And she loved the way his dark hair shimmered in the early morning light. It curled over his ears and down to his shoulders. Reaching upward, she tucked a stray lock behind one ear. His steps slowed, and he turned his head toward her.

"What?" he rasped out.

"Ye are more handsome when ye smile."

The man frowned. "My lady, ye are with fever and should not speak thus."

Ailsa realized a part of what he spoke was true. On the morrow, she would most likely regret the foolish words she'd uttered out loud. Nevertheless, Desmond made her feel oddly strange, and no other man had ever stirred any emotion within her.

Letting out a sigh, she turned her gaze outward. "Ye are correct, Desmond. 'Tis no more than fever talk. I shall attempt to remain silent until I have recovered."

However, when she stole a glance at Desmond, his mouth twitched in humor.

Chapter Seven

"Dare to open the box of love and see all the glorious presents you could have missed."

Gritting his teeth, Desmond dodged the blasted item that had continued to strike his face for the past few hours on their journey. The offensive piece was attached to a stunning head of gold tresses, and he wanted to rip it free. Whatever brew the druid had given Ailsa had caused her to sleep soundly. In addition, her head jerked with the movement of the horse.

At least the lass had stopped talking. Her words earlier unsettled him. Though she was touched with fever, he knew her to speak her mind. Did she not say it was a failing of hers? When she had slipped her arms around his neck, Desmond fought the urge to look into her eyes. If he had, he feared what he would have done next. Ailsa tempted him as no other had done, and this bothered him greatly.

Studying more intently the comb in her hair, he almost burst out in laughter. It was a beautifully carved dragon with a gem in its eye, seeming to be staring at him from its perch. He believed the Fae were mocking him with dragons everywhere.

Shifting his position, he tried to keep Ailsa steady and leaned her head against his shoulder. Her cheek grazed his chin, soft and warm. Desmond swallowed and tried to resist the lass in his arms. The scenery was far more important. With the undeniable arrival of King John's men roaming the glen, he shook his head to rid his thoughts of the soft body he cradled.

Tam rode up alongside him. "She still sleeps?"

He arched a brow at the druid. "What was in her drink?"

Looking affronted, he sputtered, "*Herbs*...for healing and rest."

"Ye should have waited to give her the sleeping draught when we reached Urquhart."

"Agreed, but Lady Ailsa would have been uncomfortable riding with ye. I worried she would not have rested and fought the pain."

Desmond cast a disapproving look at Tam. "Is there something wrong with me?"

"Ye ken what I mean."

Leaning forward, Desmond adjusted the hood of her cloak over Ailsa's head. "Will this make ye happy? Her fever seems to have lessened."

The druid narrowed his eyes. "Call for me when she wakes."

Watching as the man fell back behind him, Desmond began to count the hours until they would arrive at Urquhart. The sooner he released his hold on the lass, the better for all their moods.

By late afternoon, snow fell heavily. As they reached the outer edges of Urquhart, they were unable to see the looming fortress. Ailsa's fever had also returned, and she moaned often. There was naught they could do, but keep moving forward. He adjusted his arm over her shoulders to keep her movements slight.

Alastair held up his hand. Bringing his horse to a halt, Desmond waited. The man dismounted and bent on one knee, examining the area. Raking a hand through his hair, the Dragon Knight walked over to him.

"Horse dung on the path. 'Tis not fresh, but I dinnae want to risk the chance of encountering King John's men. Though it may be a lone traveler."

"Another way?"

Alastair glanced upward. "Aye, but we shall not make it by nightfall to Urquhart with the weather."

Unease slithered inside Desmond. If they took shelter under the trees, he feared for the safety of the lass. "Ailsa's fever has returned."

The others had gathered around Desmond and heard his words.

Tam moved his horse near his. Reaching outward, he placed two fingers on Ailsa's forehead. She trembled in Desmond's arms. "We must seek shelter for the Lady," urged the druid.

"There is another way. If the storm abates, we can journey along the loch and come in behind Urquhart. Give me a few moments and I shall return," stated Alastair.

Desmond nodded and pulled his own cloak around Ailsa. He gave no care for the outraged look on Muir's face. If he wished to see his lady stay alive, he had to trust her into his keeping. He looked to her father. The drain of the battle and his own injuries showed on his face, but the determined look of a warrior held firm within in his eyes.

Reaching for his ale skin, Desmond passed it to the MacDuff. The man regarded his offer for a moment and then took the skin. Taking small sips, he handed it back. Extending the courtesy to Muir and Tam—each took a swig. Desmond took barely a sip and attached the ale skin to the front of his horse.

Moments slithered by and snow fell more heavily. Each man kept his gaze shifting around the area. Ailsa let out a groan as she moved within his arms. Now was not the time for the lass to wake. Sensing his animal's frustration, he eased the reins and kept his focus on where Alastair departed.

The Dragon Knight appeared quietly from beneath the trees. Rubbing his hands together and stomping his feet, he quickly mounted his horse. "I have sent a message to my brothers, Duncan and Angus."

"How is this possible?" demanded Muir.

Alastair ignored the man. "Duncan can ease the snowfall, and Angus will meet us near the northern end of the loch. He can bring forth the light."

"Again, I ask ye—"

Alastair glared at the man. "I sent a wolf to Urquhart." Turning around, he moved forward down the hill. "My wife will convey the messages."

"My sister can speak with the animals, as well," added Desmond. Seeing Muir's stunned look, he turned away to hide his own mirth. Giving his horse a nudge, he followed Alastair.

Hearing Tam do his best to explain to Muir about the Dragon Knight's powers caused Desmond to chuckle. Recalling his own encounter with the man when he arrived one morn in Eire with his sister, he could fathom why Muir had a difficult time believing Alastair could speak with the animals.

As for himself, Desmond was grateful for the

A Highland Moon Enchantment

Dragon Knight's gift. He feared another night in the harsh elements, and Ailsa, though strong, would worsen.

"Wo...*wolf?*" She shivered in his arms.

Desmond leaned near her head. "Aye. Alastair can speak to the animals. He has sent a message to Urquhart for help."

"Wh...why?" she sputtered out and then added, "Body hurts."

"Go to sleep," urged Desmond, trying to maneuver them down a narrow path between the trees.

"Too hot," she murmured. "I should be on my own horse."

"Nae. Rest, Ailsa."

She grumbled something Desmond couldn't understand and then became quiet. Saying a silent prayer she would remain so, he continued to move at a steady pace. The brittle air stung his face, but he gave no care. Keeping his focus on the path and trees, he let out a sigh, as her head slumped forward. *Sleep, lass.*

Snowfall and the sound of horses surrounded them on their journey. Onward they continued until the gray sky crept into early night.

When his horse stumbled into a snowdrift, the sting of cold on both their legs roused Ailsa.

"Get me off," she protested weakly.

Biting back a curse, he firmly kept one arm around her.

She started to struggle. "Let...go."

"For the love of Brigid, be still, Ailsa, or we will tumble off my horse."

"Then ye get off," she muttered.

Desmond was tempted to halt and have Tam give

her another sleeping brew.

Finally, the area opened up and the loch appeared before them. "Thank the Gods." Chafing his nose on his arm, he guided his horse downward. Making their way along the edge of the loch, they picked up their pace as the snowfall abated.

Smiling, he realized the wolf had reached Urquhart. Within an hour, light glimmered in the distance and relief coursed through Desmond. Angus came forth from the trees, brightness glowing around him and his horse.

"Praise the Gods and Goddesses," proclaimed Tam.

"How much farther?" asked Bran, moving past the druid.

Desmond studied the man. "Through the trees and up a narrow incline. Angus is the leader of the Dragon Knights."

Bran straightened fully. "We have heard the tales of the Fire Dragon."

Angling his head at the man, Desmond asked, "Good or bad?"

"Honorable."

"No…fi…fire," mumbled Ailsa, shaking her head.

Bran removed his glove and reached across to touch her face. "Sweet Brigid, ye are burning up."

"She will be in good care when we reach the castle. There is a healer among the women," assured Desmond.

The man shifted on his horse. "Good. I have nae wish to bury my daughter along with her mother."

As Angus approached, he had words with Alastair. Then, lifting the ball of light farther around them, he motioned for everyone to follow. Desmond had never witnessed the use of power by Angus, though he had with Alastair on many occasions. He marveled at the magic of the Fire Dragon within the man.

Onward their group traveled along the water. Curving to the right they cautiously made their way up the small incline. Nearing the top, one of the horses slipped, but Alastair was able to steady the animal before moving ahead to the top.

As Desmond came up beside him, Alastair reached over and placed a hand on the animal's nose. Muttering soothing words to Desmond's horse, he chuckled. "Aye, soon ye shall have food and warmth."

Once again, Desmond witnessed the power Alastair MacKay had with the animals.

Bran and Muir gathered around them. The glow of Urquhart lit the night sky—a beacon to the weary travelers, and Desmond urged his horse forward. The dull ache in his left arm, which began several hours ago, he shoved aside. The warmth of the castle called forth and renewed energy filled him.

Entering through the portcullis, Duncan's son, Finn, and the stable master, Tiernan greeted them. Soon, Duncan and Stephen came out, speaking with Alastair as he introduced Bran, Muir, and Tam.

Angus approached him. "Give me the lass, so ye can dismount."

Desmond did his best to ease her off gently, but she groaned when he carefully handed her to Angus. Quickly dismounting, he stretched out his arms, and took Ailsa back.

"What happened?" asked Angus, gesturing him to move ahead.

"They were attacked by a few of King John's men."

"Where?"

"Not far from Aonach."

"Bastards," uttered Angus with contempt.

"Down," rasped Ailsa. "Sick."

Desmond placed her feet on the ground, but held her firmly. "Can ye walk?"

She shook her head and promptly threw up on his boots. "I am sor…sorry. Head and back hurts."

"Shh…" Lifting her back into his arms, Desmond noticed Angus staring at him.

"There were none to tend to her. They suffer from their own injuries," he divulged, glaring back at Angus.

Angus brushed a hand over his beard. "Wait here."

Watching as the Dragon Knight went to the well, Desmond let out a groan as the man returned with a bucket of water and dumped it onto Desmond's boots. "How kind of ye, Angus."

As they entered the castle, Angus departed for the Great Hall where the rest of the men had gathered.

Fiona rushed to his side. "Aileen and Deirdre are preparing a room for her. Alastair explained what happened. Follow me."

Slowly making their way up the stairs and along a corridor, Desmond followed his sister into a chamber. A fire blazed in the room, but it did naught to cast off the chill. "Can ye build up the blaze?"

"No, Desmond. If she has a fever, we don't want the room to be stuffy. She'll be comfortable under a light cover," assured Aileen, placing a hand on the woman's head. "Greetings, Lady Ailsa. My name is Aileen, and I shall be tending to you."

"The druid gave her a brew this morn. She has drifted in and out of sleep."

Aileen snorted and tossed her braid over her shoulder. "If she had not eaten, then it will make her feel this way. I'm shocked she didn't become ill."

"I did," interjected Ailsa. "All over Desmond's boots."

"Oh, goodness." Fiona smirked and looked away.

"Bring her over to the bed," ordered Aileen.

Striding forward, Desmond placed her back upon the pillows and she let out a cry. "Forgive me, Ailsa."

"'Tis all right," she whispered, gazing up at him.

The moment Aileen undid her cloak, she gasped. "Has she been traveling in this bloody gown?"

"Aye," stated Desmond.

"Not my blood," added Ailsa.

Fiona stepped near the bed. "Good to meet another warrior."

Ailsa smiled weakly and closed her eyes.

"And you, dear brother…" Fiona came around the other side and took his arm, leading him out of the room. "They are filling a tub for you in your chamber."

Desmond glanced over his shoulder at Aileen. "Ye will heal her, aye?" His question was one of concern and it pained him to leave her, though he could not fathom why.

"I never make promises, but I will do my best," she replied, smiling.

He raked a hand through his hair and nodded.

Looking down at his sister, she arched a brow in question at him.

Pulling her along out of the room, they moved silently to another set of stairs and corridor. She paused before his door and placed a hand on his chest. He waited patiently for her to speak, but she shook her head.

"I had no wish to see the lass die," he blurted out.

She batted her eyes. "Did I *say* anything?"

Before he could speak, she opened the door and shoved him inside. "Bathe, put on some fresh clothes, so the next time you see the *lass*, you'll look presentable."

Desmond fisted his hands on his hips. "Dinnae start to tell—"

The door to the chamber slammed shut, not giving him a chance to finish his retort.

Chapter Eight

"Be careful not to trample the faery flowers emerging forth from the snow."

As Desmond descended the stairs, Muir stood leaning against the entrance to the Great Hall. The man eyed him steadily as he approached. Pushing away from the wall, Muir blocked his path.

Desmond regarded the man in a calm manner, though in truth, he wanted to shove him aside. "Did ye wish to speak to me?"

"I am grateful for your aid, but since we have sought shelter at Urquhart Castle, ye can leave off seeing to Lady Ailsa."

Weary from the journey, Desmond found he had no words for a retort. However, frustration seethed inside him. "Anything else?"

"Only that ye heed my words."

Curious, he asked, "Why? I have done naught to your lady. Merely protected and seen her safely to Urquhart."

Muir stepped closer. "Remember my words, O'Quinlan."

Desmond surveyed him coldly. "Why do I sense a threat?"

Stephen appeared by his side. "Have ye eaten, Desmond?"

Keeping his gazed fixed on Muir, he replied, "Nae. I was on my way into the hall."

"Do come inside. 'Tis cold out in the corridor."

Desmond nodded and stepped around the annoying man.

Entering the hall, Stephen clamped a hand on his shoulder. "We must teach ye some manners, O'Quinlan."

Desmond halted and looked at him. "Have I done something wrong?"

"I am simply jesting with ye," chided Stephen and released his hold. "Did ye ken Muir is kin to clan Donald, though he is a Cameron? Bran mentioned it to Angus."

"Nae. Is he from the Isle of Islay?"

Stephen kept his voice low. "Did not say. Claimed he is a guard for the MacDuff. Furthermore, the man seems to have a thorn up his ass. He offered no words of thanks for food or drink. Although, the MacDuff has been gracious and forthcoming with why he is here in the glen."

"Which is?"

"To scatter his wife's ashes in the loch. Moreover, he is barely a distant relation to the Earls of Fife. He did share this when Alastair questioned him."

Desmond eyed the MacDuff with curiosity. "Why would he dare to journey during this time of year? He would have fared better during late spring or early summer."

Stephen leaned near him. "A vow the woman requested on her deathbed to bring her here immediately after her death."

"Strange request to give to her kin," muttered

Desmond.

"Agreed. Yet, I believe the man is sincere."

Stephen took a seat and gestured for Desmond to sit near him.

Sitting down across from Alastair and Duncan, he reached for a jug of wine. Filling his cup, Desmond listened to the talk between Angus and the MacDuff. When the mention of King John's name entered the conversation, Angus' eyes blazed with fury, and he fisted his hands upon the table.

"When the weather lessens, I shall send a messenger to King William. Again, King John tries our king's patience with these skirmishes. It angers the people, especially learning his men have moved deeper into the glen," stated Angus.

"Is King William nearby?" asked Muir as he took a seat next to the MacDuff.

"Aye," responded Angus. "He makes his way here to celebrate the Midwinter feast with us."

Bran leaned forward. "Truly?"

Angus nodded slowly and reached for the jug. Refilling the MacDuff's cup, he added, "We would be honored if ye remain here at Urquhart to join us in the festivities."

The MacDuff straightened and took his cup. "Ye honor us by your invitation. In truth, we had told our people we would not be returning until after Midwinter. They understood the journey we faced."

Alastair pushed a trencher of food toward Desmond. Filling a bread bowl with the warm venison stew, he paused. "I am sorry to hear the news of your wife's death."

Bran MacDuff gave him a curt nod, but showed no

sign of emotion. "She was a great woman. All suffered from her passing."

Desmond dunked his bread into the stew and took a bite. "As I am sure your daughter, Ailsa, felt keenly her loss, as well."

Muir gave him a scathing look, but Desmond ignored the man and turned his attention back toward the MacDuff. "My sister and I suffered cruelly at the loss of our parents."

"As we all have here," commented Alastair.

"Where do ye hail from?" inquired Desmond. Reaching for his cup, he drank deeply.

Folding his arms over his chest, Bran eyed him curiously. "As ye were not present when I told the MacKay, we come from the Isle of Ailsa Creag."

Desmond's hand stilled. Now he knew why the lass' name had bothered him. He remembered his mother speaking of the place. Mystical and ancient, the place was shrouded by the mists of the ocean and land. "I recall the stories from my mother of your home."

The MacDuff arched a brow. "Bards weave many a tale throughout the land."

"Even as far away as Eire," added Desmond, refilling his cup.

"Then she was of the old beliefs?" asked Bran.

"Aye," he replied softly.

"As was my wife. Her people came from Eire, as well."

Fiona entered the hall with Merlin, Alastair's wolfhound, trailing behind her. She gave her husband a smile and walked over to Bran. "Your daughter is resting. Our healer, Aileen, has revealed she has not broken any ribs. However, she has suffered heavy bruising, and has a small fever. With *rest*, she will recover swiftly. Tam is also with her. She has requested to see you."

Bran's mouth twitched in humor at Fiona. "I can assure ye it will be difficult for the lass to remain in bed for verra long. Her stubbornness is a trait among the MacDuffs."

Fiona gave a sidelong glance to Desmond. "Stubbornness can be a strength *and* hindrance."

Desmond glared at his sister. Though, relief had coursed through him the moment he heard his sister proclaim the news about Ailsa.

"I shall go speak with the lady," announced Muir, rising from his seat.

The MacDuff held up his hand. "Nae. She wishes to see her father."

For a moment, Desmond feared the man would argue with his chieftain. Nevertheless, he nodded and took his seat.

Bran rose from his chair. "Lead the way, Lady Fiona."

"When ye are finished, permit me to share a cup of *uisge beatha* before ye retire to your chambers," stated Angus.

"Thank ye," replied the MacDuff.

"I believe I shall take my leave," commented Muir. Rising from his seat, he gave a curt nod to Angus and strode out of the hall.

As soon as the doors closed, Duncan folded his arms over his chest. "Why do I sense unease with Muir?"

Desmond snorted and continued to eat his meal.

"Ask O'Quinlan," suggested Alastair, chuckling

softly.

As Desmond lifted his head, all the eyes of the MacKays were on him. Letting out a curse, he replied, "I carried his woman on my horse, and he took offense."

Stephen coughed loudly into his fist. "I see a fight coming in the lists."

"Are ye sure she is to marry this man?" asked Duncan.

Shrugging, Desmond reached for the jug of wine. "He behaves like a man who has claimed the woman. I did what I thought right at the time. Her father had a broken arm and head wound. Muir also suffered from a blow to the head. It left only me to tend to the lass."

Duncan narrowed his eyes. "And yet, ye did not think to have Alastair carry the lass on his horse?"

"O'Quinlan took immediate charge of the woman," interjected Alastair.

Desmond growled and drained his cup. The wine left a bitter taste in his mouth.

"Enough," demanded Angus. "They are now our guests and ones who have suffered with the loss of family and men." Turning toward Desmond, he arched a brow. "Will there be a problem with ye and this man?"

Offended by the MacKay's question, Desmond stood. "There will be nae problem. I shall stay away from *your* guests."

"O'Quinlan," warned Angus. "Ye take offense at my meaning, where there is none."

Tired and weary, Desmond let out a frustrated sigh. "Forgive me. I shall see ye all in the morn."

Uncertainty filled him as he left the hall. For the

remainder of November until after Midwinter, he had to remain with people who left him frustrated and confused. Frustration with the Dragon Knights and confusion over a certain blue-eyed lass.

Striding out of the castle, the blast of icy air slapped his face, and he welcomed its sting.

****

"No more," Ailsa protested, shoving the spoon away. "I can tend to myself."

"Like you did last evening? Wincing from the pain, you spilled the contents in annoyance. And Fiona, who is with child, cleaned up your mess," responded Brigid, sitting on the edge of the bed. "Must we once again remind you that you have suffered bruised ribs? You're fortunate they did not break and puncture a lung."

Ailsa grimaced and met the hard stare of the woman. Her eyes reminded her of another. They mirrored the same color and arch of brow. However, this was not her beloved mother. She considered three days in bed was enough, though the pain continued to weaken her. Relaxing her shoulders, she lifted her head. "I will accept your help for one more day."

Brigid smiled. "Agreed. And in the morning, you can sit at the table by the window." She dipped the spoon into the broth and held it before Ailsa's mouth.

Ailsa allowed Brigid to feed her, though her insides screamed to do it herself. "I did not ken Fiona is with child."

Waving the spoon in the air, Brigid replied, "Yes, and Aileen, too."

Taking another bite, Ailsa's eyes went round. "'Tis good to hear new life abounds here for the Dragon Knights."

Smiling, Brigid added, "Yes, indeed."

Frowning, Ailsa shifted slightly. "If I may ask, ye and the other women speak in a strange language. 'Tis the words of the English, but not the tone. Furthermore, ye use words I cannae fathom. Ye are not of this place."

The woman's hand stilled over the bowl. "You perceive much, Ailsa. How much do you know about the MacKay Dragon Knights—their history?"

Ailsa sighed and closed her eyes. "My mother has shared the stories since the verra beginning of the Order." Opening her eyes, she continued, "They were descended from the Fae and bestowed powers from the elements. We ken about their magic, since our isle is a haven as well. We had heard of their downfall and then rise once again to take their place as leaders. Our druids spoke of the curse. They also mentioned of the women who traveled the stars to save their souls. Are ye from those stars?"

Brigid put the bowl on the table. "They were not cursed. It was a prophecy for them. A *quest* for each of the brothers. On each of their journeys, a woman was sent through the Veil of Ages, sometimes guided by a Fae warrior."

Reaching out, she grasped Brigid's hand. "Ye..." She swallowed. "Ye have traveled from another time?"

Nodding slowly, Brigid squeezed her hand. "I'm sharing this knowledge, since I have a feeling you will understand."

Ailsa released her hand and leaned back. "'Tis incredible. *My* home is on an island on the southwest of Scotland. Generations have taken refuge within our rocky isle. Most of the time, the mists encircle the land, protecting us from invaders. We have no wish to venture off the island. 'Tis a place where we also train warriors in the old ways. We have sent two men to be with the Fianna."

Brigid's eyes went wide. "You should speak with Deirdre and Angus. They traveled with the Fianna, before coming home to Urquhart."

"Truly?"

"Yes. Your father mentioned you were traveling to the loch to scatter your mother's ashes. I am sorry to hear of her passing. I lost my parents when I was young, so I do understand about loss."

Ailsa felt comforted by the woman's words. "Her last request was to be with the Great Dragon."

Beaming, Brigid stood. "She is a marvel to behold."

"Do ye think she will be present when the time comes?"

Brigid touched her cheek. "I will ask her."

Ailsa gasped and reached for the woman's hand. "Ye can do so?"

"All the wives of the Dragon Knights speak with her. She holds great wisdom and is a good listener. If not for her sage advice, I fear I might have traveled another path." Brigid squeezed her hand and then released it.

Sighing, Ailsa leaned back against the pillows. Her mother had spoken about the wonder of the last dragon, but she never fathomed she would witness the beautiful being. "Thank ye, Lady Brigid."

"Please call me Brigid."

Smiling, she replied, "Only if ye call me Ailsa."

"Deal."

Ailsa laughed, but immediately regretted the

action. Wincing from the pain, she placed a hand on her side. "Do ye think I can sit on the chair by the hearth?" She gave the woman a pleading look.

Chuckling, Brigid placed the bowl onto a nearby table. "All right. But let me grab Deirdre or Aileen to help, too."

"I can assure ye—"

"Yes," interrupted Brigid. "I know you're a strong warrior woman, but you're shaky when you attempt to stand. I don't think your father will be pleased if I tell him you fell and broke a bone. Or my husband, if you fell on me."

Both women turned at the soft tapping on the door.

Brigid went and opened the door. "Good morning, Desmond."

A thrill of excitement shot through Ailsa. She had been told the man had asked morn, noon, and eve about her over the past several days. Though he never entered her chamber, she recalled hearing his deep voice last evening.

"Perfect timing, Desmond. I was on my way to have one of the other women help move Ailsa to a chair by the hearth."

"No need to bother them. I can assist the lady."

Brigid glanced over her shoulder at her. "Will that be agreeable to you?"

Ailsa held up a hand. She hastily tucked a stray lock of hair behind her ear, and folded her hands in her lap. Giving the woman a nod, she waited.

Opening the door wide, Desmond stepped inside and walked toward her. He gave her a slight bow. "Good morn, Lady Ailsa."

Her mouth became dry, and Ailsa found it difficult

to form any words. It was as if she were seeing the man for the first time. Gone was the heavy beard, though the shadow of one remained. He wore a fresh tunic and trews that hugged muscular legs. Her face heated, and she quickly looked away from those glittering green eyes.

He stepped closer. "Are ye still with fever?"

"Nae," she blurted out and lifted her head.

She thought his smile could disarm a wild boar, and Ailsa melted right there on the bed. He leaned forward and lowered his voice, "'Tis good to hear. Take hold of my left arm, since your injuries are on the other side. Ye can lean on me."

Ailsa nodded, his breath warm against her face. A mix of honeyed bread and ale.

Placing her hand on his strong arm, he helped to lift her with the other one. Standing on shaky limbs, she waited. "Can we move, please?"

His eyes held mirth when he replied, "When ye stop shaking, I will help ye move forward."

"Afraid I'll collapse into your arms?"

"I would welcome the fall," he uttered softly.

By the hounds! Were his words a challenge? Her face heated even more, but strength seeped into her bones.

Taking a step forward, Desmond helped her across the chamber to the chair. She sank into the deeply cushioned seat. "Blissful."

Surprising her, Desmond reached for her hand and placed a kiss along the knuckles. "My pleasure, Lady Ailsa."

Brigid approached, tucking a fur covering over her lap and under her feet. "There. I'm sure you'll enjoy some time away from your bed, sitting by the hearth."

As Desmond turned to leave, Ailsa called out, "Thank ye, Desmond, and please call me Ailsa."

When he glanced back over his shoulder, he gave her a smile that sent her heart racing. Ailsa feared she was coming down with a fever once again.

Chapter Nine

"Listen to the sparrow's song at daybreak, and embrace the winter morn with a melody in your heart."

Leaning against the pillar, Desmond watched Alastair deflect the blows from Muir. The man had been intent on practicing in the lists within the first few days of his arrival. He boasted his injury would in no way keep him from sparring with a Dragon Knight. Though Muir had strength, Alastair had more within him. On occasion, the Dragon Knight's dragon would slip to the surface and once, he noticed fear in Muir's eyes.

"Ye would have thought he would have learned a lesson with Alastair on the first day," mentioned Duncan, handing Desmond an ale skin.

Desmond took a sip. "It has been seven days and the Cameron attempts to use the same tactics against Alastair. He believes he can tire man *and* beast."

Duncan rubbed a hand over his jaw. "And ye ken well they do not tire easily."

He shot him a cold look. "Nae. They only become angrier."

"Aye. His beast has been known to rule the man. Nevertheless, your sister has managed to tame both."

Handing the ale skin back to Duncan, he said, "As I have witnessed."

"Brave man to fight a Dragon Knight once again," uttered Bran coming alongside him with Ailsa on his arm.

Desmond straightened from the pillar. "Should ye be venturing out into the cold air, Lady Ailsa?"

Bran flashed him a look of disdain. "My daughter's welfare is none of your concern. Lady Aileen and our druid have assured me the fresh air will do us both some good."

Ailsa rolled her eyes. "Must ye be so harsh, Father? The man was simply making inquires. Or are ye upset because he did not mention *your* health?"

A shadow of annoyance crossed Bran's face, but it quickly vanished. Casting his gaze outward at the two men sparring, he asked, "How long have they been out here?"

"Since dawn," replied Duncan and handed the ale skin to the MacDuff.

"Goodness." Ailsa shook her head. "Is Muir trying to defeat Alastair?"

Duncan coughed into his fist, trying to contain the laughter. "Only a fool would believe he could."

Bran smiled, and Duncan gestured them over to a bench. Desmond remained standing by the pillar. When Ailsa glanced over her shoulder, confusion marred her features. "Will ye not join us?"

Desmond shook his head. "'Tis better I stay away from your father's ire, Lady Ailsa."

Sighing, she strolled back to him. "Did I not tell ye to call me Ailsa? Ye are as stubborn as my father."

His mouth twitched in humor. "So I have been told."

Ailsa laughed softly. "So your sister has informed

me, as well."

He squeezed the back of his neck. "I must have words with my sister about discussing my bad habits."

Ailsa moved closer and placed a hand on his arm. Her presence surrounded him, and Desmond found he could not move. The morning air was brisk, but he found himself burning from her touch.

"Please do not scold her. She is with child and suffers from illness in the morn. Your words might upset her." Smiling, she added, "If it helps, she also speaks kindly of ye, too."

Swallowing, he could only nod. Even in his sister's current condition, Fiona still could cut out his heart with her words and toss his own right back at him. "Ye are feeling well?"

She brought the fur-lined hood of her cloak more firmly around her head. "Aye, thank ye. However, it will be another week or two before my father or Aileen allows me to enter the lists."

Desmond found himself staring at her face. He could no longer hear the words she spouted as she continued to speak. Her face was as white as the snow-covered ground they stood upon. Yet, it was those lips he was drawn to—full, red, and when her tongue teased along her bottom lip, his heart slammed against his chest. What would they taste like? Blinking several times to rid himself of the lustful vision, he glanced away.

Suddenly, he recalled her mentioning the lists. "Ye train? A woman? For what?"

She stiffened and shook his arm. "Have ye not heard anything I have been saying? Our isle is one of training. We have several men now traveling with the

Fianna. I am a chieftain's daughter who will one day rule. I train alongside the men *and* women of our clan. We honor the old ways. Furthermore, my father has spoken of our home with the Dragon Knights. Were ye not present?"

Desmond stared at Ailsa as if seeing her for the first time. "Pray forgive me. I did not fully ken his meaning. Most evenings, I seek the shelter of Angus' scrolls, or pass the time playing fidchell with Fiona."

Her frown turned into a beaming smile. She grasped his arm. "Ye play the game?"

He was helpless to resist and placed a hand over hers. "Aye. My sister is a quick study. She also plays chess with Alastair, though I have yet to capture the meaning of the moves."

"By the hounds, I have missed the game of fidchell. 'Tis one my mother taught me. Tam enjoys the game too." She leaned nearer as if she was going to impart a great secret to Desmond. "Though I must confess, the druid lacks the skill of attacking one's adversary. I long for a good challenge."

He leaned near. "Then I accept your *challenge*."

She burst out in laughter. "Ye may regret those words, Desmond O'Quinlan."

"Remove your hand!" shouted Muir.

Snapping his gaze to the man, Desmond removed his hand. "It would seem as if I have offended your man, Muir."

"He's an overbearing brute," spat out Ailsa.

Frowning, Desmond stepped away from her. "Does he not have claim on ye?"

"What?" Her question was laced with disgust. She pointed a finger at Muir. "*Him?*"

"Aye, the Cameron."

"Nae!"

Watching as Muir approached, fury etched across his face, Desmond gave him no time to utter another word. Stepping forward, he leveled a fist to the Cameron. "Quit telling me what to do," he clipped out angrily.

****

Ailsa stared at Desmond's retreating form. She almost burst out in laughter when he thought she was intended for Muir. Her eyes followed him until he disappeared around the stables.

"Bastard," growled Muir.

She quickly averted her gaze and looked at her guard sprawled out on the ground. "I find your behavior unjust. Desmond did naught wrong."

Her father and the Dragon Knights had gathered around them.

Muir wiped the blood from his mouth and stood. Pointing a finger at her, he snapped, "*He* had nae right to hit me. *He* put his hands on ye! I merely defend—"

Ailsa held up her hand to stay his words. "Desmond O'Quinlan has shown only honor. And if ye must ken, I put *my* hand on his arm first."

Bran let out a soft curse.

She turned toward her father. "I am not a weak maiden who needs protecting. I wish ye—"

"As ye have often stated," her father interrupted.

"Let us retreat to the Great Hall. I am sure Desmond will make his apologies once tempers have cooled," suggested Duncan.

Ailsa took a step to the side. "I will follow shortly. My temper cannae be cooled inside."

Her father gave her a skeptical look, but nodded and walked away. Muir shook his head, yet, kept his tongue, and followed Duncan out of the lists.

Crossing her arms over her chest, she stole a glance at Alastair. "Are ye not joining them?"

Smirking, he asked, "Would ye like me to show ye where Desmond went?"

Her face heated, but Ailsa's gaze never wavered. "Aye. I would be most grateful."

As the Dragon Knight led her out of the lists, he veered sharply to the left away from where she saw Desmond take his leave.

"We are not heading to the stables?"

"Nae. The O'Quinlan retreats often to this place when he's upset." Alastair paused and glanced over his shoulder at her. "He longs for his home, I believe."

"Then why does he not return?" she asked, ducking under a pine limb as they made their way down a narrow path on the other side of the stables.

"My wife deemed he should stay on until after the Midwinter feast."

Shocked by his words, Ailsa paused. "She would wish him to leave during winter? To travel all alone to Eire?"

"'Tis not what ye think." Alastair halted and pointed ahead. "Follow the path, and ye will find Desmond. If ye wish to have your questions answered, ye must ask him."

"Thank ye," she said, stepping past him.

Making her way out of the cluster of pines, the view of the loch opened for Ailsa. The scene from above was mystical. The mists hugged the snow-covered hills, but it was the water that called out to her.

Peaceful and calm, it rippled down the glen in soft waves. No wonder her mother wished to be scattered here.

Ailsa drew back the hood of her cloak and sighed.

"'Tis a beauty, aye?" asked Desmond in a low voice.

The burr of his words skimmed across her skin, and when she cast her gaze on him, his eyes held hers as he leaned against the bark of a pine. The look he gave her sent a tremor of excitement through her body. Regaining her self-control, Ailsa swept her sight back to the loch.

"I have no words. We have many rivers and streams on our island, but this is vast."

She heard him move away from the tree and step beside her. They watched as a flock of geese glided above the water, making their way south. Sunlight broke free from one of the clouds—its light glittering over the water like tiny jewels.

"Why are ye here, Ailsa?"

She shrugged and then asked, "Did ye injure your hand on the man's face?"

Desmond roared with laughter—rich and warm.

Ailsa stared at him in wonder. Gone was the solemn and serious Desmond O'Quinlan. In his place was the man who stole her breath. Never before had another captured her attention and she longed to find out his secrets. He was much too severe. He needed to laugh more often.

"Ye should smile and laugh more," she suggested and turned away from him.

"Aye, true. Furthermore, I thank ye kindly for your concern, but my hand is nae damaged."

She eyed him hesitantly, and then reached for his hand. Though calloused, it was warm and strong. Ailsa traced her fingers over the top, noticing the redness. He flinched as if she burned him. Lifting her gaze to meet his, she said, "Pack some snow along the ridge, and ask Tam for comfrey. The cold will ease the swelling and—"

"The herb will help the bruising," he concluded, smiling at her.

Returning his smile, she quickly glanced away. "May I ask a private question?"

He leaned near her and lowered his voice. "It would depend on how private the question might be."

Ailsa shivered and clasped her hands together. "I meant only to ask why ye have not returned to Eire."

Desmond blew out a frustrated sigh and walked away from her. Picking up a stone, he tossed it outward. Frightened squirrels darted out from the nearby trees, and a bird screeched in obvious displeasure.

Fisting his hands on his hips, he maintained his gaze on the loch. "My sister reckoned it best I stay. She believed I had unfinished words with her husband from an incident that happened many moons ago."

"Though, will ye not miss your sister once ye leave?" she inquired, stepping near him.

He shifted his stance and folded his arms over his chest. "Aye. But we shall see each other again."

"Hmm… Well I am pleased ye did stay."

"Ye are?" He frowned, running a hand through his thick hair.

"Of course. Ye and Alastair saved us from certain doom."

"I am certain another would have come to your aid,

Lady Ailsa."

Furious, she stepped around in front of him. Poking him in the chest, she stated, "Ye cannae be so assured. And have I not asked ye to simply call me Ailsa?"

His steady look raked over her face, dark and compelling.

Finally, he took a step back and shook his head regretfully. "As I have stated once before, I have no desire to stir the wrath of your father any further. I deem it wise to return to the castle, *Ailsa*. Surely he would not like ye to remain alone with me."

"I grow tired of having to repeat myself," she uttered in an irritated tone and turned away from him. "I am not some delicate maiden who requires an escort."

"Nae, ye are not weak. But 'tis your honor that your father is concerned for."

Ailsa snorted in disgust. "He kens I can protect myself. If I want to speak with someone, I dinnae need a guard."

Desmond leaned close to her ear from behind. Ailsa could feel the warmth of his breath on her neck, and she shivered. "Ye would if someone wished to steal a kiss," he whispered softly.

His words skimmed across her face in a soft caress, and she tried to breathe. She found her body heated and her tongue frozen.

Swallowing, she turned her head to the side. The man had silently left the area. Ailsa placed her cool hands on her heated face. He had never touched her, but his words sent a longing of desire—to be kissed.

Pulling the hood of her cloak over her head, she slowly made her way back to the castle. And for the first in her life, Ailsa pondered what it would be like to have the handsome Desmond O'Quinlan crush her into his arms and steal a kiss.

Chapter Ten

"Beware the heady power of the moonlight. Her radiance will shelter any who walk in her glow."

Entering the kitchens, Ailsa halted and inhaled the aroma of fresh baked bread. She took in the scene with all the women present. Fiona and Brigid were kneading dough. Aileen stood on a stool in an attempt to hang herbs for drying, and Deirdre was chopping vegetables and waving a knife about as she spoke. Their cook Delia clucked her tongue in displeasure as she surveyed the women, and then turned her attention to a pot over the fire.

"Be careful, Aileen," chided Deirdre. "Stephen won't be pleased if he hears you've fallen off again."

Aileen gave her a warning. "Just because I'm pregnant doesn't mean I'm fragile. If you utter one word, I'll slice out your tongue with the knife you're wielding."

Deirdre laughed. "You can try, but we all know I'm more accomplished with blades."

"You're wicked. It's only a small stool. Do you want to hang the herbs?"

"I told you I would, so get down from there." She tossed a mushroom into her mouth.

"Let me hang them," suggested Ailsa walking fully inside the cozy kitchen.

All movement ceased. The only sound was the snap of flames from the fire.

"You are a guest, Lady Ailsa," stated Fiona, wiping her hands on her smock.

Her shoulders slumped. "*Please* give me something to do. I believe I have rested enough. I can move more freely. Moreover, I believe Brigid has told ye that we have spoken about where ye have traveled from, so ye can speak more freely around me."

Aileen smiled at her and stepped down from the stool. "Only if you promise to rest before the evening meal. You might think you're healed, but trust me, your body will be aching for rest by the end of the day."

Ailsa waved the woman off. "A walk within the grounds will not tire me."

"No, but if we put you to work in the kitchens, you will be."

Ailsa grimaced in good humor. "Then I give ye my promise to retire to my chamber when I am done here."

The woman winked at her and handed her the herbs. "If you would be so kind, I need all these placed on the pegs." Aileen then pointed to the stack neatly tied together in bundles on the wooden table.

"I will not require the stool," confessed Ailsa.

"Didn't think you would, since you're taller than all of the women here," teased Aileen who moved past her to pick up the baskets on the floor.

"There's more vegetables to be chopped," suggested Deirdre, giving her a smile. Walking over to her, she draped a smock over her head and tied the sides for Ailsa.

"Thank ye." Ailsa gathered the bundles and proceeded to hang the fragrant herbs. "The bread smells delicious."

"Oh, my," uttered Brigid. "Did you not break your fast earlier? I thought to send a tray up to your chamber, but assumed you would like to eat in the Great Hall."

Turning around, Ailsa smiled warmly at the woman. "Aye. Tam made sure I ate fully before I ventured out with my father this morn. I have never eaten such grand fare before."

Brigid punched the dough down. "Our men have hearty appetites."

"For *everything,* and I don't mean food," added Fiona and snickered.

"Face is flushed, Fiona. We can always tell when you and Alastair—"

"Hush, Deirdre!" she hissed out. "We have a guest."

Ailsa rolled her eyes. "Dinnae worry thus with me. I work alongside the women on our isle. In the kitchens, training, and in the fields. Although there are times when I have ventured out onto the sea with my father and a few of his men to catch fish for our people." She sighed and leaned against the table. "'Tis a glorious sight to be on the ocean. Ye can almost catch a sense of freedom while on the water."

"Your island sounds wonderful," stated Fiona. "Desmond is the only one in our family with a love for the sea. My other brothers and I prefer to keep our feet on solid ground."

"Ye have other brothers?" asked Ailsa hanging up the rest of the bundles.

Fiona dusted her hands off. Striding over to the other side of the table, she sliced into a loaf of bread Delia had removed from the oven. Taking another knife, she smeared honey over the top and held it out to her. "I have two other brothers—Niall, our leader, and Brian."

"What are they like?" asked Ailsa, taking the offered food.

A thoughtful smile curved her lips. "In comparison to Desmond?"

Ailsa concentrated on eating the warm, delectable bread. "Aye."

"Niall is a great leader. Strong, dependable, fair, and loving. The people have a great amount of respect for him. Brian is..." she paused and tapped her foot. "He is a true mediator—with men *and* women. However, Desmond is the quiet one. He loves the sea, horses, and has a restless spirit."

Ailsa glanced up. "Why?" she asked softly, wanting to understand him more.

Sighing, Fiona stepped closer. "I am getting to know my brother. After a battle was fought in our village—one where our parents died, I was taken away for my safety. I was dreadfully young. We were not reunited until a few years ago."

She wanted to ask more questions, but realized it would merely draw attention to her. Aye, she was curious about the man, but thought it best to end this particular conversation. "I am sorry for the loss of your parents."

Fiona placed a protective hand over her abdomen. "As am I. However, my journey has led me to the man I was destined to be with. Therefore, through all the pain and loss, I had to find Alastair. In addition, I found my brothers again."

"Ye are a strong woman, Lady Fiona," she uttered

softly.

The woman touched her arm. "Please, call me Fiona."

Smiling, Ailsa nodded. Licking the stickiness of the honey from her fingers, she was unprepared for the assault of two children as they came running into the kitchens with one holding a wooden sword.

"Give it back ye thief!" shouted the young lad.

The lass taunted the boy. "Nae. My turn."

"Now!" he demanded, his eyes turning colors right before Ailsa.

Ailsa watched the scene unfold as the two apparent twins, though one dark and the other fair-haired, battled over a sword.

He lunged for his sister, causing them both to tumble onto the floor.

"For the love of the Goddess, stop!" ordered Aileen, wiping her hands off and storming over to the fighting children.

"Must be the oncoming power of the full moon madness," announced Brigid, as she placed her bread into a bowl.

"Won't be full for several more days," corrected Aileen.

Removing the sword from the lass, she pulled the two children apart. Tossing it onto the table, she brought them over to a bench. "Why did you take Aidan's sword, Margaret?"

The lass lifted her head. "'Tis my turn, Mama."

Aileen gave her a piercing look. "But it's not your sword. Did not Uncle Alastair make one for you?"

Her lip trembled, but her gaze never wavered. "I lost it," she whispered.

Aileen wiped a stray curl aside. "How?"

The girl pointed to the boy. "Ask Aidan."

The lad giggled. "In the water."

Frowning, Aileen asked, "Please tell me you did not wander down to the loch?"

Aidan lowered his head, his golden locks falling forward. "Nae, Mama."

"He made the water come to him," whispered Margaret. "Then it took my sword away."

The lad glanced sharply at his sister, but kept silent.

"Sweet Mother Danu," uttered Aileen softly. She cupped her son's face, forcing him to meet her eyes. "Do you understand what you did was wrong, Aidan?"

Shrugging, he replied, "But it called to me."

"Nevertheless, it was wrong. Your father has spoken to you before, Aidan. I can see you did not listen, or did not understand his words."

The lad raised his head. "Are ye going to punish me?"

"Your *father* will consider what is best."

His eyes grew wide. "I promise never to call the water again."

"That is not why I am upset, Aidan. You used it for the wrong reason." Standing, she held out her hand to him. "Let us go seek out your father."

"Aye, Mama," he grumbled, taking her hand.

Aileen turned toward Margaret. "And just because your brother rid you of your sword does not mean you can take his."

Margaret nodded and reached for the sword off the table. "I am sorry, Aidan. Here."

Snatching the sword from her daughter's hand, she

placed it back on the table. "It shall remain here until after Aidan speaks with your father."

"Then I will watch over it for him," she pronounced.

Aileen rolled her eyes and turned toward Ailsa. "Forgive my children. As you may have heard, this is Aidan and Margaret." She turned to the children, "Lady Ailsa is our guest at Urquhart for the Midwinter season, so let us show her our manners."

Aidan made a bow. "Greetings, Lady Ailsa."

Margaret hopped off the bench. "Ye are pretty, Lady Ailsa."

"Yes, she is pretty," agreed Aileen and added, "But that is not how we greet a guest."

The lass made a short curtsy. "Greetings, Lady Ailsa."

Trying her best not to burst out in laughter, she smiled fully. Crouching down next to them, she took each of their hands into hers. "I thank ye for the welcome. Please call me Ailsa."

Margaret looked up at her mother. "She is pretty *and* nice."

Aileen smiled and softly replied, "Yes, she is."

All heads turned as loud shouting erupted from outside the kitchens. Instantly, Desmond darted inside with a laughing child within his arms and a wolfhound trailing behind them.

"And the hero, Cuchulainn unleashed the hounds on his enemy, forcing his foe to remain standing on the hill," Desmond uttered in a firm voice, swinging the young child high in the air.

"Hells bells," muttered Brigid smiling.

Ailsa stood slowly. This man was a different

person. His hair fell across his forehead, giving him a younger and untroubled look. The boy patted his uncle's cheeks tenderly. Desmond caught her gaze and gave her a lopsided smile. Suppressing her own merriment, she cupped a hand over her mouth.

"Goodness, Desmond. Must you tell him fighting stories? The babe is barely sixteen months," his sister chided.

Handing the squirming babe to Fiona, he shrugged. "Ye ken he likes my tales. Helps to soothe the beast within. Yet, he favors the ones with animals, too."

"He appears older," observed Ailsa. Reaching outward, she tousled the child's dark curly locks.

"All the children look older than their years," replied Fiona. "They walk at an early age, talk, and show signs of their powers." She nodded toward Aidan. "As you witnessed with the twins."

"A marvel," murmured Ailsa.

"You wouldn't think so when they're throwing a fit." She placed a kiss on her son's cheek. "This one has been known to rattle a room with his power of the land."

"And don't forget when we found him in the Great Hall with all the horses," added Deirdre.

"Truly?" asked Ailsa.

Fiona laughed. "Yes. He can speak with all animals. His gift is more enhanced, since I carry the gift, too." She pointed a finger at Deirdre. "But her son, Alexander, has the power of fire and has singed a few of us in a fit of anger."

"It will take prayers and patience to keep Urquhart from crashing or burning to the ground while trying to raise these Dragon Knights," uttered Deirdre. "At least we have no worries with Margaret, our wee healer in training. Or the older ones—Nell and Finn who are Brigid and Duncan's children. They show no signs of creating havoc."

"Would you like to hold Hugh? I want to finish my bread," asked Fiona.

Smiling, Ailsa nodded and reached for the babe. Instantly, he grabbed one of her braids and started to play.

"No, Hugh. Do not pull so hard," ordered Fiona and placed a reassuring hand over his chubby one.

"'Tis fine. He is happy," said Ailsa. Staring into his green eyes, she made a face. The babe let out a chuckle and promptly shoved her braid into his mouth.

Desmond roared with laughter and pulled the end free. "Ye will find nae pleasure in eating her hair, wee Hugh."

"Mama, can I fetch his toy to chew on?" asked Margaret.

"Yes, dearest," replied Aileen, making her way out of the kitchens.

Ailsa chuckled and moved to the bench away from the others. "He is charming."

"Aye, when he is in a good mood." Desmond leaned back against the table.

She cast him a sideways glance. "Are ye saying ye fear the babe?"

"Nae," he uttered softly, placing a gentle hand on Hugh's back. "I only fear the battle ahead he faces with his own beast that dwells inside."

"He has strong kin here. They will assist him." Ailsa bounced the babe on her knee.

Desmond bent and placed a kiss on Hugh's head.

"Aye, along with the O'Quinlan clan. He has calmed being in your arms. Do ye like children?"

Ailsa's face heated as she gazed into Desmond's eyes. She had never shared her longing to have children. Not even with her mother. How could one profess wanting children, but find it difficult in finding the right man? Sadness filled her, recalling her father's vow to see her married upon their return. She sighed. "Aye. I like them."

Smiling, he rose from the bench. "Ye will make a good mother one day, Ailsa."

Her heart pounded as she watched Desmond walk out of the kitchens. She could not fathom the ache within her, but in her heart, Ailsa would not settle for anyone. It was all for love or naught. She would fight her father until her last breath.

Fiona wandered over and placed an arm on her shoulder. "I have found my brother is quite fond of children. Our brother Brian boasted that once Desmond stated he wished to have as many as ten bairns."

Ailsa gaped at the women. Did she not profess the same under a full moon when she was young? She snapped her gaze back at the entrance to the kitchens. "Goddess help the woman he marries. Especially if they are all girls."

"Most definitely, since they will have him tied in knots with constant worry."

Both women burst out in laughter.

Chapter Eleven

"Cup your hands under the light of the full moon and cast out your heart's desire."

"If ye continue to stare at the lass, I fear her father will take a blade to your eyes," muttered Alastair, poking him in the ribs.

Desmond's body stiffened in shock. How long had he been watching Ailsa? He found himself drawn to her as she ate, laughed, argued, and debated with the other women. For the past several days, he longed to hear her voice and see her face. She loved being around the children, and the women had embraced her, especially his sister. Earlier in the day, he had come upon them in the lists. Ailsa was showing Fiona a new angle with the bow and arrow. His sister was good with the weapon, but with Ailsa's help, she mastered the skill far better than he had done.

He was bewitched by Ailsa's charms, and he rubbed a hand over his face. Looking around the table, Desmond noticed Bran and Angus had removed themselves away from the main table and were speaking near the entrance of the Great Hall. Shoving his trencher of food away, he made to stand.

"Are you leaving, Desmond?" asked Fiona. "I thought you would be interested in a game of fidchell?"

Glancing over his shoulder, he gave her a look of

confusion. "Ye wish to play?"

"No. I have an ongoing game of chess with Alastair. I thought you'd want to show Ailsa the game. I've told her how you made it out of wood, instead of the customary leather or stone."

Desmond looked at Ailsa. "Are ye not tired?"

She smiled. "I dinnae believe *one* game will tire me. Did ye not mention a game last week?"

"Aye, but my duties have kept me away."

Alastair choked on his mead. "Ye have none."

Desmond gave the Dragon Knight a scathing look and then quickly averted his gaze to Ailsa. "I will go fetch the game."

Hastily making his way out the hall, he all but ran up the stone stairs. Entering his chamber, he retrieved the game from a table by the arched window and tucked it under his arm. Making his way back down, he found Ailsa seated in the corner by the hearth. Glancing around the hall, Desmond noticed they were alone, and he halted near the door. Her golden hair shimmered in the firelight, and he found himself lost in her beauty once again.

"Are ye going to stand there all evening?" she asked, gesturing for him to sit across from her.

As he made his way to the table, he noticed two cups filled with wine. "Ye will need your wits when ye play the game," he stated, placing it on the table.

She laughed, the sound warming him all over. "Desmond, I do believe ye have challenged me with your skill."

His mouth twitched with amusement as he set the board down and pulled forth a small leather pouch. Placing the game pieces on the board, Desmond sat down.

Ailsa brushed her hand over the wooden board. "'Tis a beauty with all the carvings along the edges. If Tam sees this, he might put in a request for ye to fashion a board."

"And not ye?"

A rosy glow spread across her neck, and Desmond longed to see how far it extended. "I did not wish to be so forward. Besides, ye would have nae time with all your duties," she replied softly.

"Since the moment we have met, ye have spoken your mind," he countered, leaning forward on the table. "Dinnae start to play coy now."

Ailsa averted her gaze and picked up one of the game pieces. "Where did ye find the white and blue colored stones?"

"A gift from Fiona," he answered, leaning back in his chair. "She heard I had lost several pieces and with the help of the other women, searched along the loch. They spent an entire day looking for exactly the same size and colors. Even Brigid's daughter, Nell, helped in the search."

"Your sister is verra kind and has a gentle spirit." Ailsa placed the piece back on the table. "Ye may be the king and defenders."

Desmond shook his head slowly. "Nae, my *lady*. Ye shall be the queen. I will attempt to storm your defenders."

She pulled on her bottom lip with her teeth. "Ye wish to capture me?"

By the hounds, aye! He wanted to capture her lips and plunder her mouth with kisses. Desire shot through his body, and his cock swelled. Reaching for his mug,

Desmond drained the contents. "Aye," he stated in a firm voice, keeping his gaze locked with hers.

Ailsa reached for her cup and drank fully. "I like a good challenge," she responded, placing her finger on one of her stones.

"Why have ye not married?" Desmond asked, waiting for her to make the first move.

Startled by his question, her hand stilled. "Why must I? Can I not rule without a man by my side?"

Desmond arched a brow. "I merely wished to inquire why no one has claimed your hand."

Her finger moved one of the pieces forward. "There have been many."

Scanning the board, he countered with a move. "Too old? Too young? Too fat? Thinning hair?"

She snorted. "Aye—all of those and a desire to *control* me."

His expression grew serious. "Ye are a woman who does not require a firm hand."

Ailsa's smile quickly faded. "Ye might want to mention that to my father. Upon my return, he has insisted to see me wed. And most assuredly to someone who wishes to see me as an ignorant wife."

"Then I shall pray ye find one who does not," he uttered softly. "Your move."

And for the next few hours, the battle was fought, with the aid of more wine. Desmond found Ailsa to be an expert opponent. When she had eluded his capture on more than one move, she teased him with a smile that would bewitch even a hardened warrior.

As the hour grew late, she gave a slight yawn. "Shall we continue tomorrow?"

"Of course."

However, Desmond had no wish to part from her. His mind screamed to stay rooted in his chair, but his body betrayed him. Standing, he reached for her hand. "I will escort ye to your chamber."

She eyed him with curiosity and stood. "Nae. Take me to the north wall. I hear the view of the loch is one that steals the breath from your lungs."

"Done." When her fingers slipped into his, Desmond fought the urge to crush her to his chest. Placing her soft hand in the crook of his arm, he led her quickly out of the hall and up the stairs. Bending to the left, he took her along a corridor and up a narrow circular pathway. The torches flickered as he approached the door leading to the north wall.

A cold draft blew by them, and she shivered. Instantly, regret filled him realizing he had not considered to bring a cloak for her.

Desmond paused by the door. "Ye should not venture out into the biting cold without a cloak."

Her eyes narrowed. "I simply wish to capture a quick look, not spend the night sleeping out there."

Shaking his head, he pushed open the massive oak door. Brittle air slapped at his face while they made their way up along the wall.

"'Tis cold," she muttered, but chuckled softly and hugged his arm. "But ye are warm."

"We shall not tarry long," he assured her and placed a warm hand over hers.

"Oh, sweet Goddess. Look at the moon, Desmond. Her light shimmers over the water. I have now witnessed the charm of the loch in sunlight *and* moonlight. Though our rivers are stunning on their own, they cannae rival this view. As I have told ye, our island is shrouded in mists, so ye cannae see verra far out into the sea."

Desmond's focus was not on the moon, but the beauty standing beside him. To take what he dared not possess. He marveled at her delight of the striking scene.

Ailsa turned toward him. "Thank ye, Desmond, truly."

Her nearness was overpowering, seducing him in a way he had never known. Desmond cupped her chin. Her eyes widened, and her lips parted in invitation. Moonlight and lust danced within her eyes. No longer did he battle with his mind and body, and he slowly lowered his head.

And under the silent whisper of a full moon, Desmond captured her soft lips within his own. He could taste her sweetness mixed with the wine, and desire shot through his veins. His hands shook as he placed them securely on her waist. As he deepened the kiss, she placed her hands around his neck. Desmond groaned, crushing her body against him.

When his tongue sought hers, she drew back, breathing heavily.

He released his hold. "I am—"

Ailsa placed a finger to his lips. "Nae. Teach me how to kiss."

Desmond's groin tightened in pain. "Ye have never been kissed?"

"Stolen kisses when I was a young lass, but nae. Not from a man."

He slowly backed her up against the wall. "Then let me show ye how a kiss can burn the blood in your body." Desmond traced a finger down the side of her neck. "And how a touch can send tremors coursing through your skin." He traced a path over her bottom lip with his thumb, and she trembled under his touch. "Are ye sure ye want to learn?"

Ailsa's chest rose and fell with each breath she took. "Aye," she reassured him, placing her fingers into his hair.

In that moment, Desmond lost himself with her touch, and he let out a low growl. Capturing her mouth once again, he feasted lightly on her satin lips. Her mouth tasted divine—spices, wine, and her own sweet scent. Giving his hunger free rein, he eased his tongue into the soft heat of her mouth and teased her. Soon, she was playing the dance of desire with her tongue, and he groaned.

He deepened the kiss, and his hand trailed a path over the top of her breast. Her skin was smooth to his touch. Ailsa moaned, and Desmond allowed his fingers to move from the softness of her skin to the material that covered her taut nipple. When he pinched the bud, she whimpered. Drawing her closer, he slanted his mouth to take more of her full lips, his senses spiraling out of control.

Breaking free from her lips, he teased a path down her neck. "Ye smell so verra good," he rasped out.

"More," she urged, surprising him by cupping his face and kissing him with reckless abandon. Desmond allowed her to take the lead, even as his hands roamed down along her waist, longing to strip the gown free from her body. Nudging her legs apart with his knee, he moved against her. Fire burned through his veins, and he ached with a need to be deep inside her.

The cold wind slapped at them, but their passion

blazed all around. Desmond desired to lift her into his arms and carry her to his chambers. To make love to this woman—explore her body and give her pleasure. To tease those places that would drive her wild with need.

Instantly, his mind screamed at him. *Ye are thinking of bedding a virgin?*

Desmond jolted backward and drew in a ragged, icy breath. When Ailsa reached out, he took another step back. "Nae," he protested in a strangled voice.

"Ye are afraid to show me more kisses?" she asked, brushing her hands down her gown.

"Aye."

Ailsa took a step forward, her eyes glazing in the moon glow. "Why?"

Desmond leaned against the edge of the wall, his cock straining to be free. "Because I desire to take more than kisses from ye."

Her eyes slowly lowered, noticing his desire. Thinking this would scare the lass, he waited for her to step away. Yet, when her gaze lifted, her smile left him weak.

"What if I wanted to learn more?" she whispered, stepping closer. She placed a hand upon his chest. "Would ye deny me?"

Desmond found himself shaking and clenched his hands. "This is not a game," he growled. Taking her hand, he placed it over his cock. "My need is fierce."

She gasped, but made no attempt to free her hand. "And what about mine?" she challenged.

Never in all his life had Desmond met a woman so headstrong and stirring. Though the air around them was brittle, beads of sweat broke out along his brow. He had to make her understand what she was asking. Removing her hand, he leaned near her ear. "Would ye wish to give up your maidenhead?"

Ailsa's face transformed from one of passion to shock. She hugged her arms around herself, as if noticing the cold air for the first time. Stepping away from him, she glanced up at the moon. "'Tis a wondrous beauty. I shall always treasure this moment."

Desmond moved forward. "Let me escort ye to your chamber."

She arched a brow skeptically at him. "Nae. I fear it would not be wise."

He inclined his head. "Sleep well, Ailsa," he uttered softly.

"Ye, also."

Watching her retreat through the oak door, Desmond let out a frustrated breath. He raked his hand through his hair as he turned outward and gripped the stone ledge, trying to wrestle free from his desire for Ailsa.

They both came from two different places. One day she would rule an island. Did not she state her father wished her to wed upon her return? Perchance the man had already chosen another from among her people. Desmond considered it would serve her best if her father chose a husband who would not force her to cower behind him.

And yet, he had almost taken the woman to his bed. Claiming what was not his to take. In their lust-filled passion, she would have surely given him her body and regretted the deed afterward. He recoiled at the thought of stealing the one item she would take into her marriage bed.

Lifting his head to the full moon, he vowed to stay far away from the enticing Ailsa MacDuff.

Chapter Twelve

"The maiden believed the moonstone would protect her heart from love, but the gem only enhanced her desire."

Entering the kitchens, Ailsa spied Brigid's daughter speaking with a dog near the hearth. Moving forward, she grabbed a smock from a peg off the nearby wall. "Good morn, Nell."

Rising, Nell beamed up at her. "'Tis a fine morn, Lady Ailsa."

She rested her hand on the girl's shoulder. "Nae, only Ailsa."

The girl nodded and dipped a piece of bread into the pot hanging over the open fire. Bending back down, she presented the morsel to the animal. "What do ye think?" she asked his opinion.

Ailsa folded her arms over her chest and watched the scene unfold. The dog thumped his tail in obvious pleasure. "He seems to enjoy the treat."

Nell stroked his ears and stood. "Aye, though Cuchulainn reckons too much salt."

"Truly?"

The dog let out a sharp bark.

Nell pointed to him. "See. He agrees with me."

"Ye are a wonder, Nell."

"Yes, she is, but I think Cuchulainn has sampled

more than his fair share," noted Brigid entering the kitchens. Placing a basket of fresh herbs on a worktable, she gave her daughter a warning look.

"He was hungry, Mother," argued Nell.

Brigid brushed off her hands and pointed at the dog. "Cuchulainn is one of the most well-fed animals at Urquhart. And by the looks of him, I believe he could lose a pound or two."

Instantly, the animal lowered his head.

"Mother, please. He can hear ye," protested Nell and placed her hands over his ears.

Brigid knelt on one knee. "I am positive you can assure him I meant no disrespect, and he knows how much I love him." Giving the animal a scratch behind his ear, she stood. "Now, unless you want me to shoo him out of the kitchens, quit feeding him the venison broth."

Nell let out a sigh. "Aye."

"Why don't you both go over to the work table and chop some vegetables. There you can feed him the end pieces."

The girl smiled fully. "A wonderful plan. Come help, Cuchulainn."

Ailsa watched the pair saunter over to the worktable. "She is charming, Brigid. Her gift is a wonder."

"It continues to grow each year, along with all her animals—be they furred or feathered—that she rescues. I still will never forget the time right after we met how she tended to a wounded wolf. My heart nearly stopped beating as I watched her help the trapped animal out of its cage."

"Oh, goodness, I did not ken she was not your

blood kin. Was Duncan married before?"

Brigid gestured her over to the other side of the kitchens. Reaching for a jug, she asked, "Would you care for some water? Or would you prefer ale?"

"Water would be fine, thank ye." Taking a seat, Ailsa watched the woman grab two mugs and fill each.

Brigid handed her one of the mugs and took a seat across from her. "First and foremost, I consider Nell my daughter—as if I birthed her into the world." She glanced away. "Duncan found her and Finn soon after Duncan's sister was killed. A tempest of a storm was brewing across the land. Both lost their families during those days. Duncan became their protector and guardian." Brigid turned her gaze back to Ailsa. "I suppose fate has a way of placing those in a path where they are needed. For you see I cannot bear any children. Therefore, when I married Duncan, Nell and Finn became mine, as well."

Ailsa placed a fist over her chest. "I am sorry to have caused ye pain. I did not realize..." Her voice trailed off, and she took a sip of the cool liquid.

Letting out a sigh, Brigid placed a gentle hand over hers. "There is no need for an apology. I was blessed with two amazing children. I have no regrets."

Smiling fully, Ailsa glanced over at Nell and her companion. "So Finn is not her brother?"

"No. Though he watches over Nell and sees to her protection. Finn had an abusive father and chose to run away during a storm. Nell lost her family the same night. Duncan came across both and took them with him to Castle Creag. In addition, Nell and Finn suffered greatly at the hands of the evil druid, Lachlan. To this day, Nell suffers from nightmares, yet, they are not as often as a few years ago. Furthermore, Finn spends more time with the horses and tends to retreat into a quiet place, where even Duncan cannot reach him." Brigid sighed and leaned forward. "We are grateful for Desmond. He is able to get Finn to speak and laugh more. It does our hearts good to see the slight changes in him."

Irritation seethed within Ailsa. "Children should not have to witness such violence. Moreover, they should have beauty and light—laughter and fun." She blew out a frustrated breath. "Yet, 'tis a harsh world at times."

"It does not matter the time period either. Sadly, we cannot place our children in a bubble of protection."

Ailsa grumbled, "But we can surely give them the tools to defend themselves."

"Most definitely." Brigid smiled and took a sip of her water.

"How old are they?"

"Nell is ten summers, and Finn will turn thirteen in a few days."

Pushing her mug aside, Ailsa stood. "What can I do to help in the kitchens?"

"Nothing," remarked Brigid and moved away from the table.

Gaping at the woman, Ailsa waved her hand about. "Truly? Ye ken I am nae good at sitting quietly by the hearth stitching. I have nae more aches and can move freely."

Brigid's mouth twitched in humor. "I overheard Aileen and Tam saying you were fit to resume riding your horse. They say your *beast* has been nipping at any who pass by her, so leave the confines of this place and get some fresh air."

Taken aback, Ailsa stared at the woman. "I will have ye ken Elva is an even-tempered animal. Surely she is upset with the lack of exercise."

Grabbing some herbs out of the basket, Brigid proceeded to snip a few into the large steaming pot of broth. "Obviously, she prefers to have her mistress take her out than anyone else. All the men have attempted to coax her, but she refused to budge from her stall."

"She is not used to newcomers," countered Ailsa and removed her smock. Eagerness filled her to know she was able to ride her horse once again. Her feet couldn't move fast enough out of the kitchens.

"You have been here for over three weeks. Surely that is plenty of time to adjust," shouted Brigid.

Ailsa halted. Stepping back inside, she asked. "And Midwinter?"

Glancing over her shoulder, she replied, "In two weeks."

Nodding, she quickly moved along the corridor and up the stairs. The time during her injury and getting well had flown by. Reaching her chamber, she entered and pulled forth her cloak, gloves, and dirk. Dashing back out, she hurried down the stairs and out into the bailey. Cold air whipped around her, but Ailsa embraced the elements. Sunlight splintered through the gray clouds, and she smiled. Snow had not fallen for many days, and her heart soared with the possibility of a ride along the loch.

Ailsa hugged her cloak more firmly around her, as she approached the stables. Warm laughter greeted her as she stepped inside. Her heart started to beat rapidly at seeing Desmond leaning against one of the stalls and watching Finn attempt to feed her horse pieces of kale. It was the first time seeing him in almost seven days.

For reasons she could not fathom, Desmond had stopped taking his meals with everyone else. He simply vanished after their evening on the north wall. Her lips still burned at the memory of his touch, but she quickly banished the image. Apparently, the man had regrets and wished not to be around her.

Steeling her emotions, Ailsa glanced at the lad. She knew the morsel would never tempt her horse. She preferred other fare and this was not one of her favorites.

"Elva favors hard oatcakes, cabbage, fennel, and apples," proclaimed Ailsa, moving fully inside the stables. Keeping her focus on her horse, she brushed past Desmond.

"Good morn, Lady Ailsa," greeted Finn, stepping aside.

"Aye, 'tis a fine one." She stroked the animal's forehead tenderly. "I have some good news, my lady. We can venture out for a ride today."

"By whose order?" demanded Desmond.

Ailsa tried hard not to roll her eyes, but failed miserably. "I need no one's consent."

"Ye ken 'tis not safe with your injuries," the man argued.

Finn eyed her skeptically.

Smiling, she kissed Elva's nose and turned back toward Finn. "If ye would be so kind to help me ready my horse, I will be grateful. Ye will find Elva will be more agreeable after some fresh air."

The lad looked past her in an obvious attempt to seek approval from the man.

"I will help, *Lady* Ailsa," remarked Desmond in a low voice.

Finn shrugged and tossed the kale into a nearby basket. Muttering something to Desmond in passing, she heard him chuckling as he departed the stables.

Biting back a curse, she tapped her foot impatiently. Refusing to meet Desmond's glare, which she surely knew was displayed across his face, Ailsa waited. When several moments ticked by, she stole a glance over her shoulder. Her anger simmered below the surface when she saw him tending to his own horse.

Storming over to him, she fisted her hands on her hips. "What are ye doing?"

"Preparing my horse. If ye are to venture out of the castle, ye must have another to safeguard ye. It has not been so long since ye were healed."

"Perchance I should ask Muir, since I cause ye such displeasure." Abruptly turning around, she stomped over to Elva. Tossing off her cloak, she thought it best if she tended to her own horse.

Before she had a chance to lift the latch on the stall, strong arms twirled her around. Desmond kept his hands firmly locked on her arms, and Ailsa fought the urge to kick the man. Her gaze collided with his forest-green eyes.

"What gives ye leave to speak thus?"

He was far too near, invading her space and smelling of leather, horses, and all male. "Why are ye so angry, Desmond?"

He blinked in confusion. "I gave ye no assumption. Now answer my question."

"Ye have not set one foot inside the Great Hall in over seven days. Have I offended ye? Was I simply another lass to woo kisses upon? Or are ye always biting out your words as sharp as your sword?" she blurted out unable to contain her own fury.

He lessened his hold, and the minutes ticked by. Ailsa saw the conflict within his eyes. "I cannae be near ye," he muttered.

She feared asking the question and turned her head away. "*Why?*"

Desmond released his hold when voices spilled forth from outside the stables. He placed a shaky finger to her mouth. Pushing past her, he unlatched Elva's stall. Watching as the man made steady progress preparing her horse Ailsa remained silent. When he was finished, he handed her the reins. She quickly put on her cloak and waited for him.

Leading his horse out of the stall, he pushed open the main stable doors. Looking about, Desmond finally gestured her to follow him outward. Without a word, he took her hand and helped her onto her horse. He then quickly mounted his own and proceeded to move forward out of the bailey and through the portcullis. Nodding to two guards, he took off hastily down the path along the loch.

Fearing pain, Ailsa kept Elva at a slow and steady pace. Yet, after several moments, she relaxed, feeling joy at being outside and riding her horse. A tree limb smacked at her face, and Ailsa laughed. She gave a nudge to her mount, and the horse picked up her speed. Soon they were galloping alongside the shore. Freedom infused Ailsa.

Casting her sight out toward the loch, she watched as the geese flew gracefully over the ripples of the water. Directing her gaze back toward Desmond, she maneuvered her horse upward along a worn trail. Onward they traveled through the trees. Sunlight filtered down through the canopy of branches, and Ailsa slowed her horse. Soon they rode up along a ridge, and she shielded her eyes from the sun's glare.

Spotting Desmond beneath a cluster of large oaks, she slowly made her way toward him. He had dismounted and stood staring out at the water below. His profile was one of quiet strength. But earlier, she had witnessed something else—a battle she fought herself. *Lust.* She ached to be with Desmond. Furthermore, it was more than wanting to be with the man. Ailsa found she could be herself with him. Aye, in the beginning, he treated her as a weak damsel, but no longer.

Dismounting, she gave a firm pat to Elva. "Do not get friendly with his beast." Watching as her horse let out a snort and trotted away, Ailsa stepped near the man. The wind whipped at loose strands of her hair, and she tucked one behind her ear. Not one for being patient, she found it difficult to form any words to get him to speak, since her own tongue was twisted into knots.

"I find I cannae control myself when ye are near," he uttered quietly, moving toward Ailsa.

She let out a shaky breath as he now stood mere inches in front of her. "What do ye wish to do?"

Desmond let out a growl and placed an arm around her waist. "This." Lowering his head, he captured her sigh with his mouth.

Ailsa shivered, her body overcome with fire as he took his other hand and splayed it across her breast. His tongue thrust deep—stroking hers, and she clutched at his tunic. Desire hummed in places she did not know existed, making her crave more. Desmond made her feel things she never dreamed of wanting.

Gently breaking free, he traced a finger along her bottom lip. "I want ye every waking moment. Does that answer your earlier question?"

She swallowed and cupped his cheek. "Ye cannae hide forever."

Sadness filled his eyes. "Nae. But I can until ye depart." He took a step back and coldness slashed between them.

Realization dawned on Ailsa as surely as the sun set each day. They may desire one another, but each would leave for their own homes. Torment and confusion battled inside of her. Wiping a hand across her brow, she turned away. "As always, ye are correct." Staring at the vastness of the place, Ailsa went and leaned against an oak.

Shocking her, Desmond strolled over to her side and cupped her chin. He smiled weakly. "Not always."

Ailsa tapped his chest. "Ye have honor, Desmond O'Quinlan."

"I find I am losing all sense of myself when I am around ye." He placed a feather-like kiss on her lips. "And I believe it would be wise if Muir escorts ye outside the gates of Urquhart when ye wish to go riding."

She angled her head. "Then why did ye this time?"

He released his hold and placed his hands on either side of the tree, trapping her against the rough bark. His eyes darkened. "To steal one more kiss. To taste what I cannae ever have. I may have *honor*, Ailsa, but I am a man as well. I find myself losing control with ye."

"I will always treasure your kisses, albeit longing for more," she uttered softly.

A devilish look came into his eyes. "Ye tempt fate, Ailsa."

Her face heated. "I have done so all my life. It would seem—"

Letting out a curse, he captured her mouth silencing any further discussion.

Her senses sizzling, Ailsa gave herself into his keeping, demanding more as she stroked her tongue against his. His groan filled her body as she wrapped her arms around his neck. Aching in places she didn't understand, she moved against him. Heat rippled underneath her skin, and she yearned to remove her cloak. "Too warm..." she murmured against his rough cheek.

Desmond broke free, his breathing labored. "Kisses like those will set your body on fire."

She chuckled low. "I have never felt this way with another. I want to touch your skin with mine. I want..." Ailsa wiped a hand over her brow.

Desmond captured her hand and placed a kiss along the vein in her wrist. "What ye wish is something I desire, too. However—"

"But we cannae," she interrupted and moved away from him. Yet, Ailsa ached for something more from Desmond other than his body.

He stepped near her. "Now ye ken why I must stay away."

A dull ached throbbed behind her eyes, and she rubbed at her temples. "Storm is coming."

"Ailsa?"

Barely hearing the man calling out to her, Ailsa

slumped to the ground, holding her head. Shards of pain pierced her mind like blades, and she bit back a curse. "Don't…un…understand."

Desmond's warm arms encircled her body, lifting her into his embrace. "Shh…*mo ghrá.*"

Did he just call me his love? Ailsa leaned her head against his shoulder, drifting into a black chasm of pain.

Chapter Thirteen

"To safeguard his heart, the warrior used his honor as a shield."

Storming through the gates of Urquhart, Desmond brought his steed right up to the massive oak doors of the castle. Duncan was the first to greet him, a frown marring his features. "What happened?"

"She was rubbing her head and spouting feeble words about a storm coming. And then she passed out."

"Give her to me," ordered Duncan.

Placing Ailsa's limp body into the Dragon Knight's arms, Desmond quickly dismounted. Seeing Finn, he waved him over. Placing a hand on the lad's shoulder, he asked, "Can ye go up to the ridge and fetch Elva? In my rush to return, I left Ailsa's horse behind."

Finn nodded. "Aye. I shall bring something to tempt her as well."

"Thank ye."

Turning to Duncan, he took Ailsa back into his arms. "Please send for Aileen or Tam."

Duncan rubbed a hand down the back of his neck. "Aye, but I believe I ken what happened. Take her to her chamber, and I will send for them."

Confused, Desmond fought the urge to demand more from the man and barely nodded. Stepping past him, he made his way into the castle and up the stairs.

Entering her chamber, he gently placed her on the bed. Unfastening her cloak, he brushed a hand over her brow.

"Will ye not wake, lass?" he urged, clutching her hand.

Duncan soon entered. "Nell has gone to fetch Aileen and Tam. They went in search of mistletoe for the Midwinter feast."

"And her father?"

"He was in the stables. If ye have any sense, ye would remove your hand and stand apart from Ailsa."

Desmond cut him a sharp glance. "I have done naught."

The man shrugged. "'Tis your death."

Blowing out a frustrated breath, he kissed her fingers and moved away. "Ye stated earlier ye might ken what is wrong? Would ye care to share?"

Duncan moved toward the window. "I believe the lass has the gift of sensing oncoming storms." Turning around, he crossed his arms over his chest. "Apparently, Tam had mentioned to Aileen about his lady's gift, though he has not been forthcoming with details. He also pointed out her father does not accept her skill."

"But why would it cause her pain?" Desmond glanced back down at her still form. Her face had taken on a pale color, reminding him of fresh snow, and he longed for her to wake.

"I cannae say until I speak with her."

"What did ye do to my daughter?" bellowed Bran, storming into the chamber.

Desmond glared at the man. "Naught. She spoke of a storm coming and then fell ill."

The MacDuff flinched, his face transforming from outrage to shock. Moving away from Desmond, he went to his daughter's side. Clutching her hand, he stared down at her. "Has someone sent for Tam, or your healer?"

"Aye," answered Duncan. "I shall go lend my services in the search."

Bran wiped a hand over his brow. "Come back to me, daughter," he pleaded.

Seeing a pitcher of ale on the table, Desmond went and filled a mug. Returning to the man's side, he handed it outward. "Has this happened before?"

Taking the offered drink, Bran shrugged and stared for several moments into the mug. Finally lifting his head, he took a swallow. "Truth be told, I cannae say for certain. I have ignored the fact my daughter has…a rare gift. I refused to listen and forbade her from speaking thus."

"Why?" asked Desmond, pulling a chair near the bed for the man to sit.

Bran cast him a look of outrage, but then quickly looked away. "This gift of sensing storms is one which is passed down from father to son. It comes from my late wife's kin, not mine. The druids' prophecy states all should bear the talent within the first-born male child. If none is conceived, then the power will pass on to the next generation. My wife and I were blessed with only a daughter, but I refused to accept she held the gift." Sighing, he handed the mug back to Desmond. Grasping his daughter's hands, he squeezed them. "How I wish her mother was here to guide her. I have been foolish all these years."

Finding it difficult to say any words of comfort,

Desmond placed a hand on the man's shoulder. "Ailsa is strong. She may have inherited her gift from her mother, but she learned her strength from ye."

Bran nodded and kissed his daughter's hands. "Aye, and her stubbornness, too." Releasing his hold, he stood. "Not only are ye brave, O'Quinlan, but I sense ye would have made a fine warrior on our isle."

Startled by the man's declaration, Desmond had no time to respond as Tam and Aileen entered the chamber. Both men moved out of the way, and Aileen went to sit on the edge of the bed.

"What happened?" asked Tam, pulling out some herbs from his pouch.

"She complained of pain in her head and mentioned a storm was coming," answered Desmond, striding over to the hearth and putting on an extra log.

"Umm...oh, goodness," stammered the druid. His gaze went to Bran. "I am sure 'tis merely a feeble headache."

Bran rubbed vigorously at his eyes. "Nae, Tam. I have known for some time that when ye say a tempest is brewing, I ken the information is from Ailsa and not ye." Glancing back at his daughter, he added, "Has she always had severe pain?"

Obviously stunned by his chieftain's statement, Tam shook his head. "No more than slight, and never has she fainted."

Seeing Duncan standing at the entrance of the chamber, Desmond strode over to him. "Give me your speculation," he uttered low.

Duncan pulled him out of the chamber and into the corridor. The torches flickered, their shadows dancing eerily around them. When he spoke, the Dragon

Knight's eyes shimmered with the beast inside of him. "I cannae say for certain, but since I am holding back the storm, it might be causing an ill effect on Ailsa."

"And your reason?" he hissed out, shifting slightly.

"I am unable to disclose them at this time."

"MacKay," growled Desmond.

Duncan grabbed him by the shoulders. "Trust me, *O'Quinlan*. 'Tis best ye do not ken."

"And Ailsa? What about her?"

"If I am correct, then the lass will awaken after I lessen my hold on the approaching storm. When she does, send for me."

Desmond raked a hand through his hair. "Do what ye must, and swiftly."

The man turned to leave, but halted. Glancing over his shoulder, Duncan said, "Tread carefully, Desmond, for I fear your heart is beginning to show for the lass. This may end badly, considering ye and she depart separately after Midwinter."

Watching as the man strode quietly away, Desmond leaned against the wall. Since the moment he encountered Ailsa MacDuff, he had battled his mind and body over the lass. He had thought it to be merely lust, but when he lifted her lifeless body into his arms, Desmond knew there was more than just his wanting to bed her. Fear at losing her, struck like a blade to his heart.

And this frightened him.

Stepping away from the wall, he wandered back inside the chamber. For the first time in his life, Desmond longed to have what the Dragon Knights had all possessed. *Love.*

Reaching for another chair, he brought it outside

Ailsa's chamber and sat. Not content to sit idle anywhere else, he reasoned his place was beside the woman who had breathed light into his soul. And once she awakened, Desmond would tell her.

****

Sharp pain slammed into his side, and Desmond blinked in confusion, trying to focus. Sitting on the cold stone, he noticed the upturned chair off to the side. "God's blood!" he roared, staring upward at the man.

"Ye *dare* to slumber by the lady's door? Did ye plan on ravishing her when our druid departed?" Muir spat out. Crouching low on the ground, he held a blade in front of Desmond's face. "I should slit your throat where ye lay."

"But not before I slice your balls from your body," growled Desmond, leveling his blade low in front of the man's body.

"Or I impale ye in the back with my axe," added Alastair from behind the man.

Muir's face paled.

"Sheath your blade, Cameron," ordered Alastair.

The man complied and stood. "Bran shall hear of this."

"And I will tell him how ye drew your blade to do harm within the walls of Urquhart," countered Alastair, lowering his axe.

Giving Desmond a scathing look, Muir stormed away.

Alastair righted the chair and took a seat. "Go seek your bed O'Quinlan."

Looking at Ailsa's closed door, he shook his head. "Nae."

Grumbling a curse, Alastair stood. "Then fetch

some food and drink."

Wiping a hand over his unshaven face, Desmond asked, "What is the hour?"

"Dawn."

"And she has not awakened?"

The Dragon Knight smiled. "Hours ago. The druid is sitting with her."

Relief coursed through him. "Has Duncan been informed?"

"Aye. He's taking his meal and then will speak with the lass."

Desmond took a seat and folded his arms over his chest. "Then I shall wait for him."

"For the love of Mother Danu," groaned Alastair. "Have ye—"

Desmond held up his hand to halt the man's words. "Dinnae speak any further. I have no wish to hear the thoughts of another Dragon Knight."

"Lugh's balls! Are ye still sitting here like a forlorn pup?" asked Duncan, striding forth.

Narrowing his eyes at the man, Desmond ignored the question.

Duncan leaned against the wall.

"I shall take my leave," announced Alastair, chuckling softly down the corridor.

"Should ye not knock?" asked Desmond.

"I am waiting for Brigid. She is bringing some broth for the lass." Duncan shifted his stance. "What did ye do this time to stir the wrath of the Cameron?"

Stretching his legs to relieve the tension from being cramped most of the night, Desmond replied, "Apparently, the man did not like finding me near Ailsa's door."

"Hmm… I find it odd the Cameron continues to find fault with ye."

Desmond pointed a finger at him and stood. "Aye! The man has nae manners and tosses out barbs at every chance."

"Perchance he sees ye as a threat to Ailsa?"

Shrugging off the possibility, Desmond understood there was naught between Muir and Ailsa. As far as Ailsa and him? "There is naught between us."

"Your actions deem otherwise," argued Duncan.

Swallowing, Desmond paced along the corridor, not wishing to pursue the conversation.

"Go seek your bed or food, O'Quinlan."

"After ye have spoken to Ailsa." He glared at the man, daring him to challenge his decision.

Brigid approached carrying a trencher. "Good morning, Desmond. I trust you slept well in this drafty corridor?"

"Aye, most assuredly," he lied, stepping aside to let her pass.

She laughed softly and looked to her husband. "Would you be so kind as to knock on the door?"

Brushing a kiss on her lips, he complied.

Tam greeted them. "Good morn to ye all."

As they all entered, Ailsa was sitting on a chair near the hearth. Color had returned to her face, and she gave Desmond a knowing smile. He returned the gesture with one of his own and stood off to the side of the door.

"When you're ready, I've brought some of Delia's broth with chicken and mushrooms," stated Brigid, and placed the trencher on a nearby table. "Would you like more water? Ale?"

Ailsa stood. "If the men are staying, then I shall need some ale, please. Are we expecting my father?"

"He is breaking his fast and will be along shortly," responded Duncan, taking a seat by the hearth.

Brigid moved toward the door. "Then ale it is."

"No need. I have brought a pitcher," announced Bran, stepping past her. "I thought we could use some, since Duncan has shared with me some knowledge as to why ye have been suffering from your gift."

Clasping her hands together, her eyes grew wide. "Ye...*ye* have spoken to the others about me? What I can sense?"

Setting the pitcher down, Bran rubbed his forehead. Lifting his gaze to meet hers, he nodded. "Can ye ever forgive me for my harsh ways with ye, daughter?"

Ailsa let out a strangled cry. "*Father!*" Rushing to his side, she embraced him.

"I have been a fool, Ailsa. I should have done more to accept what ye are. I see I have wasted time ignoring what ye have, instead of helping ye to bring it out for our clan. I shunned your gift, especially after your mother passed. I found it difficult to breathe at times. And then I feared ye were lost to me, as well."

She squeezed his hands. "Ye were...*are* still grieving. Furthermore, I am nae going anywhere." Raising an eyebrow, she added, "And as a man, 'tis challenging to ken one day a *woman* will rule the isle."

Bran tweaked her nose. "But ye are of my blood. A warrior."

She hugged him once again. Moving to the table, she poured some ale into several mugs and handed one to her father and Tam. She held another mug in the direction of Desmond. "Aye?"

Pushing away from the wall, he ached to take her into his arms. She had no idea how worried he had been. Taking the mug, his fingers brushed against hers, and he watched as her mouth parted. She quickly averted her gaze, but not before he spied the rosy blush creep up into her face. Retreating to the window ledge, Desmond drank deeply, watching as she took a seat at the small table.

"Eat," urged Brigid, sitting down across from her. The woman turned toward her husband. "Would you like to begin?"

Duncan leaned forward. "As your father has spoken to me of your gift of sensing the storms, I believe the pain ye are experiencing is my fault."

"Humph!" snorted Desmond.

Ailsa sputtered over her broth. "How can this be?"

Duncan glanced sharply at Desmond and then turned his attention back to Ailsa. "Since I have the power over the sky, I have been keeping back a powerful storm from entering the glen. I deem this has caused ye to suffer. Do ye find that once the tempest strikes, your pain lessens?"

"Aye," she whispered.

Duncan tapped a finger to his mouth. "I have another thought, which I would like to share."

Ailsa nodded. "Continue."

"I have spoken to your father and believe I can help ye to direct the storms once ye are able to sense them. If ye wish to remain hidden from the English, or other enemies, ye could use your gift to aid your people."

Ailsa blinked. "I would like some of that ale, Brigid."

The woman laughed. "Of course."

Duncan turned toward Bran. "I am curious, though. 'Tis rare to encounter another with this power. Even the druids have no more than a select few who can control the skies. Ye have spoken that it passes from mother to son."

Bran drained his mug. "Aye. It has always been thus with my wife's clan."

"And they are called?"

"The great O'Neills."

"Hells bells," muttered Brigid, dropping the pitcher and sloshing ale onto the table.

Rising, Duncan quickly made his way to her and grabbed her around the waist. "*Leannan?*"

She placed a hand on his cheek. "Strange how the fates still continue to guide us."

"What is wrong?" asked Ailsa and Bran in unison.

Desmond moved away from the window, stunned by the revelation.

Tears misted Brigid's eyes. Walking over to Ailsa, she clasped both her hands, bringing her to standing. "Remember how I told you I have traveled the Veil of Ages?"

"And a wonder," she responded slowly.

"I did not share my full name. I am Brigid Moira *O'Neill*, descended from the first Order of the Dragon Knights, which I believe you are, too."

"We are kin?" squeaked Ailsa, embracing the woman.

"Yes." Brigid laughed.

"Do ye not have the power to sense the storms?"

"Happily, no. Yet, I can speak with the Fae and sense Duncan's thoughts."

"I believe many branches of the O'Neill clan still possess some of the original power bestowed to them from the Fae, though not as powerful," stated Duncan.

"When do we begin my training?"

Duncan raised an eyebrow. "Let us wait until tomorrow. Your father wishes ye to rest one more day."

Ailsa put an arm around Brigid. "Then I am happy the fates brought us together and caused me to suffer, since this knowledge surely would have remained hidden." She glanced to her father. "Now I can truly use my gift for our people."

"Aye, my daughter," agreed Bran, lifting his mug to her.

Unexpectedly, Desmond concluded his own position within Ailsa's life. Though he had strong feelings for the lass, she was destined to become a great ruler—one who would need to choose a man from her own clan to rule at her side.

Her father may have thought himself a fool, but Desmond O'Quinlan was a bigger one to think he had a place in Ailsa's life.

The ale left a bitter taste in his mouth, and Desmond's gut soured. Quietly slipping out of the chamber, he steadily made his way out of the castle, ignoring the shouts from Fiona. He was done being around the MacKays. Finished with folly thoughts and desires.

Storming past the gates of Urquhart, Desmond took off running toward the loch.

Chapter Fourteen

"When the light of a Highland moon touches the window of your soul, there is nothing you can do but follow."

Slamming the trencher of food on the table, Fiona rubbed at her eyes. "One of these days, I'm going to throttle my brother. Stubborn, brooding, controlling, *and* rude."

"Much like my brothers," stated Alastair dryly, wrapping his arms around her waist, and nuzzling her neck.

She shivered within her husband's arms. Snuggling against him, Fiona let out a frustrated sigh. "I know I shouldn't ask, but have you and Desmond come to a truce? An understanding?"

Alastair released his hold and grabbed her hand. Bringing her to the window, he sat on the ledge and brought her onto his lap. "In time, I ken it will happen."

Fiona wrapped her arms around his neck. "So your answer is no."

He glanced out the window. "I ken ye want us to be friends, but the man is bitter. Until he seeks the reasons we cannae move forward."

"You don't have to be best buddies," she argued. Seeing his confused expression at her choice of words, Fiona added, "On good terms—close friends. I don't know why he can't be—"

Alastair silenced her words by capturing her mouth within his. Breaking free, he brushed his hands down her back. "Your brother's restless spirit is one all men strive to understand. He longs for something he has yet to fathom. He desires the verra thing I have and this makes him angry. Aye, he continues to resent me for leaving ye, but there is another ache lodged like a pebble in his boot, chafing his heart. Furthermore, he is ignorant and blindly lashes out at me."

Brushing a lock of hair out his face, she gazed deeply into his eyes. "And what is he seeking?"

Capturing her hand, Alastair placed it over his chest. "*Love*. And truth be told, I believe your foolish brother has feelings for Ailsa MacDuff."

"Are you sure it's not lustful thoughts he harbors?" Fiona tugged at the strings of her husband's tunic.

"Humph! From the moment he set eyes on the lass, he retreated farther, trying to deny it to himself. However, any fool can see the man is smitten. He watches her every movement like a hawk."

"And he did spend the entire night by her door. As if he became her protector," added Fiona softly, recalling the past few weeks as well.

"I have witnessed your brother defend his actions time and time again, not only to Muir, but Ailsa's father, too." He cupped her chin tenderly.

"Oh, Alastair, what can we do? And what about Ailsa?"

"Naught. 'Tis his own journey. We cannae push him toward something he is not ready for."

"But I have noticed the way she stares at him. Yet, I shrugged it off."

He bent and nibbled on the side of Fiona's neck. "Have ye seen the way the lass blushes when he is near her? 'Tis similar to the way your skin turns a rosy glow." He traced a tongue along the vein. "It begins along your neck and inches up to your face."

Fiona dug her fingers into his thick locks. "From the moment you strode down that hill in Ireland and rescued me, I believe I blushed for the first time."

Drawing back, he studied her face. "Ye did not fear me?"

Tracing a finger along the crescent scar on his face, she replied, "My first thought was you were a giant. My second, a powerful, *sinfully* handsome man. Fear? Never. I only feared the feelings I felt."

Sighing, Alastair glanced upward. "I am nae worthy of your love, *leannan*."

Fiona cupped his face and forced him to meet her hard stare. "Why? Because you walked out on me when you thought I was dying? You were a broken man, Alastair. You needed to heal. I will be forever grateful that in the end, you came after me." She swallowed and lowered her hands. "This is the last time we're revisiting this conversation. I sense you've been struggling with it again because of my brother, and whatever words he spoke to you."

"Ye are a wonder, Fiona. Remember, I am the land beneath your feet and will never leave ye. My love is yours...*always*."

"And I am the roots you can call your home. I will forever love you both—man *and* dragon."

Reclaiming her lips, Alastair crushed her to him.

****

As the days bled into the next, Ailsa continued to

train with Duncan. At first, he urged her to bring the storm clouds over the ridge of the mountains across from the loch. Recalling how she closed her eyes, concentrated on pulling them toward her, Ailsa burst out laughing when one white wispy cloud floated over the ridge. Scowling at her, Duncan continued to encourage, stating she had to open herself to the power of the sky. After the fourth day, Ailsa made the sky rumble with thunder, though she paid dearly with a searing headache come evening.

Her mornings were spent learning and absorbing the knowledge from the Dragon Knight. In the afternoons, she helped in the kitchens. Everyone was preparing for the feast of Midwinter, and she loved being around the other women. Furthermore, when the evening meal came, Desmond sat at the far end of the table. His conversations were clipped or in hushed tones with the other men.

Not once, did he glance her way. He behaved differently from the man she left behind on the ridge over a week ago. Confused and wary, Ailsa did not know how to approach Desmond. How she longed to go back to their simple conversations. She missed him. Perchance he no longer found her interesting. Judging it was for the best, she pushed aside all thoughts of the man.

Nevertheless, the nights left her in torment. Waking from dreams of *his* lips on her body—in intimate places she craved and where no man had touched her before. Her face heated when she recalled last night's pleasurable dream. She had envisioned Desmond entering her chamber and stealing more than kisses. His fingers trailed a path from one breast to the other, until his mouth captured them within his teeth. She awoke moaning and tingling everywhere, as if the dream had been real.

"Are you all right?" whispered Fiona, leaning near.

Blinking several times, she closed the door on her thoughts. "Aye, why do ye ask?"

Fiona pointed to Ailsa's hands. "Because you've been tearing bits of bread off for quite some time."

Ailsa glanced down to discover her trencher indeed was covered with shredded pieces of bread. Reaching for her mug, she drank deeply. "Please pass me the wine."

Fiona quirked a brow and handed her the jug. "Thirsty? Or deep in thoughts you cannot share?"

Giving the woman a sharp glance, her face heated more. "Simply thinking of what Duncan has been teaching me."

"Oh, so your thoughts were of Duncan's training. Not another?" Fiona chided and looked in the direction of her brother.

Ailsa sputtered on her wine. "I dinnae ken what ye mean," she lied.

Fiona clucked her tongue. "Desmond seems to state the same to me, too. He never understands what I mean."

Giving her a sidelong glance, Ailsa was tempted to ask what Fiona meant about her misgivings with her brother. Was there something wrong with Desmond? Finishing her drink, she placed her mug onto the table. *Be brave and ask your question.* "Is there something amiss with him?"

Fiona popped a roasted chestnut into her mouth and closed her eyes as she ate the morsel. Opening them, she stared across the table to where Desmond sat. "Yes, but I believe there is a remedy. He hasn't grasped the notion yet. He will need encouragement."

Ailsa followed her gaze. "I dinnae ken your words."

"No, but I'm sure you understand the meaning." Rising, Fiona bent near her. "Do not tarry, Ailsa. Time is a precious jewel. Don't let it vanish."

Bewildered, Ailsa watched as the woman strolled over to her husband, whispered in his ear, and then left the hall.

Slowly, she let her gaze float across the table. This moment in time was all they had. There were no promises of tomorrow. No declarations. When she left Urquhart, her life would change forever. She would rule with her father, until a husband was chosen for her. The thought made her recoil. *Why can I not choose my fate? My own husband?*

She shuddered. "Time is a precious jewel." Echoing Fiona's words softly, Ailsa stood. Angus, Stephen, and Desmond were talking about a certain path to take down to the Great Glen with her father.

Giving her father a hug, she strolled purposefully toward Desmond. Clasping her hands together, she waited for the man to acknowledge her. When he lifted his gaze to meet hers, she smiled. "We have yet to finish our game of fidchell. Would ye be too tired to continue?"

Shock registered on his face. "I believe the children have changed our original moves."

She angled her head to the side. "Then we begin anew."

"Dinnae let her cheat, O'Quinlan," interjected her

father, standing.

Ailsa shook her finger at her father. "I have never done so."

Bran chuckled softly. "Nae, not since ye were a wee lass of ten summers." Kissing her cheek, he strode out of the chamber.

She looked back at Desmond. "I will await ye at the table, so ye may finish your conversation."

Not giving him time to disagree, Ailsa quickly made her way to the other end of the hall and took her seat at the table. Noticing the mess on the game board, she arranged the pieces to their original start. Folding her hands in her lap, she sat back in her chair and waited for Desmond.

Fortunately, she did not have to endure a long wait. His presence suddenly loomed over her.

"What do ye want, Ailsa?" His tone was almost a growl.

Lifting her gaze to meet his, she replied, "'Tis no more than a game, Desmond." Though her voice betrayed her emotions.

"A dangerous one."

"Why?" she countered, quickly glancing around to find they were both alone in the massive hall.

He braced his hands on the table. "Because this is not what ye want."

"How do ye ken *what* I want, Desmond O'Quinlan?" Fury infused her words as she dug her fingers into her palms.

"Ye tempt me beyond words. As I do ye." His breath blew hot against her cheek.

Pushing away from the table, Desmond walked quickly out of the hall.

Ailsa stood abruptly. "How dare ye?" She shook, but not from rage.

Dashing out of the hall, she followed Desmond up the stairs and toward his chamber. The door had been left open, and Ailsa's steps slowed, pausing at the entrance. He stood at the hearth, hands braced against the stone above.

She eyed the line that divided the two—corridor and chamber. If she crossed over, her life would change forever.

No longer letting fear guide her, Ailsa lifted her chin and walked inside Desmond's chamber. Her fingers trembled as she silently closed the door behind her and leaned against the wood. Her fate was sealed.

His fists clenched, but he kept his gaze on the flames snapping within. "If ye do not leave, I will take ye to my bed this night, Ailsa. I will take what is not mine to claim."

Moving away from the support of the door, her legs shook. "I have nae wish to leave, Desmond. And ye need not worry. Ye are correct. My body is *not* yours to claim. 'Tis what I want to give to ye. I do so freely. To ye and *only* ye."

"Ye do not ken what ye are saying. Do ye not wish to give your body to another when ye wed? 'Tis your gift to the marriage bed."

"For the first time in my life, the choices I make are my own. I grow weary of trying to please so many. This night I am here of my own free will. If the burden of taking me to your bed is too much, then I will leave. There shall be no regrets come morning, Desmond O'Quinlan. I have nae wish to leave ye plagued with guilt."

He smacked the stone with his hand. "Then there will be none." His eyes roamed over her body as he strode toward Ailsa. Grasping her firmly around the waist, he cupped her chin with his other hand—rough, strong, and warm. "I have never yearned for another as I do ye."

"Nor I, Desmond."

With a growl, he took possession of her mouth, thrusting his tongue deep and igniting a firestorm within her body. She willingly surrendered to him, opening fully to the kiss. Clinging to his shoulders, she dueled the dance of desire with him, slanting her mouth to capture more of the man. His wild fury sparked hers, and she slipped her hands under his tunic, exploring his hard, hot, muscular body.

Breaking free, he yanked his tunic over his head and tossed it to the ground. Walking to the door, he slid the bolt into place and turned to face her. "Is this what ye seek?"

Her breathing slowed as he strode back toward her. Ailsa marveled at the man. Several scars covered his arms and chest, and she traced a path along the puckered skin. He shuddered from her touch, and she smiled, engulfed with a sense of power. Black hair dusted his chest, tapering down inside his trews. His desire was evident, and her breathing became labored. Ailsa knew what a man looked like—had heard the stories often from the other women, but never did she envision one so endowed. He was her own Angus Og, God of Love and Strength. When she lifter her gaze to meet his own, his eyes glittered like dark emeralds.

"More," she demanded.

His smile became predatory, inviting. "Your turn."

Turning around, she bit her lip. "Undo my laces?"

The brush of his fingers trembled over the back of her neck. He took his time stripping her free from her gown, stopping to place kisses along her skin. She swayed from the pleasurable sensations. When his hands pushed the material down over her shoulders, he turned her back to face him. Pulling it down over her breasts, he took his fill of her.

Cupping one breast, he blew across it. "A rare beauty."

Desmond's mouth descended, hot, and fierce, while he fondled the other breast. A low moan escaped from her lips, and she reeled from his touch. Ailsa watched in a haze of bliss as he continued to lavish her body. He trailed a path up the middle and to her neck, raking his teeth on the side.

"Take down your hair." His demand sounded hoarse to her ears.

After she removed the combs that held her tresses secure, the mass came tumbling free, and she heard his indrawn hiss. She tossed the combs onto a nearby chair and swallowed. Ailsa watched as his eyes darkened more. His desire only increased her own, and she stepped nearer.

His hand reached out and captured a lock of her hair. He twisted it around his fingers. "I have longed to see ye like thus. Ye have the most beautiful hair." He arched a sensuous brow. "I long to see the same color down below."

Ailsa splayed her fingers in his chest hairs. "Ye would?"

He placed his hands on her waist, and pushed her gown over her hips, and the material tumbled to the ground.

Slowly lowering his gaze, he smiled. "Aye." Sweeping her into his arms, he strode toward the bed and gently placed her on the furs.

Turning on her side, she watched as he removed his trews. His swollen cock jutted free, and her eyes went wide.

"Are ye afraid?" He crawled over the furs, stalking her like an animal.

Desire made her bold, not fearful. And she trusted this man. He did not seek to control, but to set her free. When she was with Desmond, the woman emerged. "Nae." She laced her fingers within his. "Kiss me again," she urged, bringing his lips to hers. His mouth tasted delicious—a mix of wine, and his scent. The kiss sent the pit of her stomach into a wild swirl.

Desmond broke free from her mouth, only to place feather-like kisses on her eyelids, cheeks, and neck. Then he slowly nibbled down to tease her breasts with his tongue. When he lifted his head, one dark lock fell forward over his eye. "But there are so many places to kiss ye."

She gasped when his fingers trailed a path down to her most private area. Ailsa squirmed under his ministrations, but he held her hips firm. He teased, nibbled, and stroked with his mouth. An unrelenting yearning ached between her thighs, begging for something she could not fathom. Desire hummed everywhere, making her dizzy.

When he slipped one finger inside her, Ailsa arched against his hand.

"Is this where ye wished to be kissed, *mo ghrá?*"

"Down...there?" Desire made her unbridled,

willing to have him do anything to her. She had never heard of this type of lovemaking, and it intrigued Ailsa.

"Aye," he growled and then plundered her with his mouth. She clung to the furs as he continued to stroke her with his tongue, igniting a fire within her blood that could not be cooled. Her breath came in short gasps, and her heart beat faster. Her body screamed for more, and she whimpered.

"Let yourself go, Ailsa. Feel my hands, my mouth all giving ye pleasure. *All* for ye." He nuzzled the words against her thigh, slipping two fingers inside her.

Lights danced before her eyes as a wave of immeasurable pleasure lifted her into an unknown abyss. Her heart stopped, and her body shattered into a million tingling pieces. Ailsa floated free, her body reeling from his touch. Desmond captured her scream with his mouth, stealing her breath, and giving it back to her mingled with his own. The castle could have burned to the ground, but she gave no care. Opening her eyes, she noticed a frown marring his handsome face. "We are not done," she uttered softly.

"I want ye more than ye ken, Ailsa. Are ye sure?"

She was lost in those green eyes—in the man who roused a passion within her body *and* mind. Words she wanted to say to him froze on her tongue, so she cupped his head and brought it toward her lips, savoring his taste and her own.

Words of endearment poured forth from him as he nudged her legs apart. Feeling his hard length pushing against her, she clung tightly to him. "Relax, *ghrá*," he urged. "It will only hurt ye slightly."

Desmond cherished her body and lips with tormenting kisses. His need so fierce, he almost spilled his seed when she touched his cheek. The moment the door to his chamber had closed, he knew their fates were sealed.

Time no longer existed. Ailsa would now be his.

Ever so slowly, Desmond guided himself into her hot sweetness, inch by inch—the torture killing him. Her scent surrounded him, and he ached to bury himself deep.

"Desmond, please," her plea came out on a sob. "I need all of ye."

He took her mouth savagely and thrust all the way inside of her. Her cry echoed inside him, and placing his hand under her bottom, he continued to move within her hot body in a steady rhythm. She fisted her hands in his hair, urging him onward. Powerful, hungry, desire spiraled through him. He was lost in a passion he had never experienced. With each thrust, each kiss, each stroke, Desmond was unable to hold back. His guttural cry of release echoed off the stones within the chamber, and he emptied all he had into the one woman he'd lost his heart to.

It was some time before either could move or speak. Gently, he rolled over onto his back and brought her against his chest. He tried to calm his racing heart as he cradled her close. Opening his eyes, he gazed upward. Troubled and confused, Desmond considered where their paths would now lead.

For the first time in his life, Desmond understood the words Alastair had spoken to him at Aonach. He loved—aye *loved* the woman he held in his arms. One night, *one* day, would not enough. Ailsa MacDuff had slipped under his skin, invading every pore, and he craved a lifetime with her.

How was it possible to let her leave when the time came?

Nevertheless, Desmond had no choice. He loved her enough to set her free. And his heart and soul splintered into a thousand pieces at the revelation.

Chapter Fifteen

"The maiden held the candle of hope within the darkness. Yet, she was blinded to the truth contained within her heart."

With the approaching of Midwinter, Urquhart Castle was thrown into a frenzied state of preparations. The MacKay women took over and gave out orders on a daily basis. Fresh rushes had been laid down, along with rosemary sprigs. Tables were arranged carefully in the Great Hall, and greenery adorned every nook—from the Great Hall, corridors, entry, and even the chambers. The intoxicating aromas from the kitchens made every man stop and beg any of the women for a morsel. Although they refused, Finn was the lone one to coax Nell into bringing out some samplings of the tasty dishes.

Grateful for the busywork, Desmond rarely saw Ailsa for several days after their lovemaking. Upon his awakening the next morn, her scent lingered, but the woman had vanished before dawn.

When he first saw her later that evening, she was strolling aimlessly along the corridor. Reaching for her hand, he shoved her into an alcove and kissed her passionately. Only when they heard voices, did they pull apart and hasten their separate ways.

Meal times were agonizing, since most of the time

they were light fare taken anywhere. Since the Great Hall had been properly prepared for the celebration they were not allowed to enter. Desmond took to eating his meals in the stables with Finn. The other men retreated to their chambers, and Ailsa took her meals with her father in his room.

Desmond foolishly thought Ailsa would seek him out in his chamber afterward, but the lass never came. Believing it to be for the best, he slept naught that first evening. He longed for her body again, and sleeping in a bed that contained their lovemaking, did naught to control his burning desire for her. Therefore, he found the hearth had become his new bed.

"Enough," he muttered and brushed the dirt from the stables off his trews.

"Here you are," chided Fiona, entering the stables with a basket.

Desmond gave a pat to his horse and walked out of the stall. "Aye, do ye have another chore?"

"No. I've brought you some food and drink. Alastair wishes you to be the first to taste his mead."

Curious, he pulled out the bench and gestured for her to sit beside him. "Why the honor?"

Fiona rolled her eyes and pulled forth a small jug, handing it to him. "He wants your opinion, since he trusts your valued input."

"Truly?" Taking the offered item, he pulled the stopper free and sniffed the contents.

"Why is it so difficult to believe?"

Desmond stared with intent at her. "Was it not ye who proclaimed Alastair and I cannae come to terms on the proportions of honey in the mead?"

She averted his gaze and dug into the basket,

producing forth a food item. "Yes, but trust me, he has never asked his brothers for their opinions."

"*Never?*" he echoed in a stunned voice.

"Nope." Unwrapping the cloth from the food, she handed it to him. "Eat."

"Hmm...nae." He held up the jug. "I must first savor this fine liquid without tainting the mead with other flavors."

"Gosh, you sound like Alastair."

Chuckling softly, he took a sip, letting the sweetness linger on his tongue and mouth before swallowing. Smiling, Desmond took another. "He listened to me."

"I take it you like the mead?"

"Aye! Most definitely. He added more honey." Placing the jug between them, he picked up the bread. "What have ye stuffed it with today?"

Leaning closer, she whispered, "I snatched a few pieces of boar and onions from the kitchens."

His eyes widened in surprise. "Is it not for the Midwinter feast tonight?"

Fiona tapped a finger over her lips. "It will be our secret."

Cupping her chin tenderly, he brushed a kiss on her cheek. "I will miss ye, Fee."

Sighing, Fiona grasped his hand and squeezed it tightly. "And I you, dear brother." Standing, she bent and kissed him on the forehead. "I've sent a tub to your chamber and having it filled as we speak."

Choking on his food, he wiped his mouth with the back of his hand. "What for?"

"Seriously? Take a look at yourself. The feast begins at sundown and you are still in the stables. You smell of animals, leather, and male. Would you not like to look your best when you dance with Ailsa?"

Before he had a chance to utter one word, she walked out of the stables, leaving him in a state of baffled shock. He never considered this was his last night with Ailsa. But come the next evening, Fenian Warrior, Ronan MacGuinnes, would come to return him back to Eire.

Suddenly, the food made him queasy, and he shoved it back inside the basket. Rising slowly, he opened the stable doors and cast his gaze to the sky. "Hear my plea, Gods and Goddesses. On our last night together, grant me this one request to have her as my own this eve. Let naught come between us. I will cherish and love her always, but give me this one last time with her, and then I shall willingly let her go."

Rubbing the ache within his heart with the heel of his palm, he went and retrieved the basket of food and mead. Securing the stable doors, Desmond left to prepare for the last feast he would ever fully celebrate.

****

"Are ye sure?" asked Ailsa, fingering the soft material of the gown. "'Tis so fine, and I have nae wish to ruin it at the feast."

"Nonsense. I want you to wear it. The pale blue color and silver trim will highlight your eyes and hair," assured Aileen as she moved a chair closer to the hearth. "Come and sit. I'll brush out your damp locks."

Nodding, she moved toward the woman and sat down. "I shall miss everyone here. Ye have all been like family with your welcoming of us." She gave out a nervous laugh. "'Tis strange to learn Brigid and I are kin. My mother must have been a seer to insist we venture to the Great Glen."

"It was your destiny, Ailsa. We have all walked the path here at Urquhart."

Ailsa reached for her mother's dragon comb from the side table. Swiping her thumb over the emerald, she bit her lower lip. If only the woman understood how her destiny was tied to another. *Desmond O'Quinlan.* Even whispering his name within her mind caused her to shiver.

She had fallen in love with him. He was her champion. Her lover. The one man she wanted by her side. Strong, smart, and an able warrior. She longed to speak with her father. But fear kept her words locked inside her heart, because of one fault. Desmond was an outsider. Her father had reminded her constantly to pick from the many clans and families on their island. He insisted there were no others and urged her to seek them out, or he would choose for her. Even her mother urged her to consider one of the men.

Nevertheless, her heart belonged to another.

Tonight was her last night here at Urquhart. Come dawn, Ailsa and her father would scatter her mother's ashes in the loch and make the journey back to their home.

Tears smarted her eyes as she gazed into the flames. Determined not to waste one precious moment of what time she had left, Ailsa would seek out Desmond. Lifting her chin, she dabbed at her eyes, refusing to let the tears fall. *I shall show ye all my love, Desmond and take what ye have to offer. Destiny can be cruel, but I will not waste a second.*

"May I put the comb in your hair?"

Aileen's soft voice startled Ailsa out of her

thoughts. "Aye."

"It's beautiful," she said, taking the item. "How fitting it's a dragon, too. It will look lovely on you."

"Thank ye," she murmured softly.

Aileen spoke no more words. She braided a portion of Ailsa's hair and secured it with the comb, letting the rest of her hair fall gently past her waist. After helping her into her gown, she squeezed her hands and stood back. "You are stunning, Ailsa. All eyes will be on you this night."

"Ye are too kind. There is beauty everywhere at Urquhart." She wrapped an arm around the woman's waist. "Let us go welcome the light of Midwinter."

Aileen smiled and gestured her forward.

Anticipation danced like butterflies within her at the thought of seeing Desmond. When they approached the steps leading downward, her father stood off to the side speaking with Stephen. As he glanced up, his face broke into a wide grin.

Stepping away from the wall, he held his hand out for her. "Ye remind me so of your mother."

Embracing him, Ailsa placed a kiss on his cheek. "Although, I have the eyes of a MacDuff, as she often used to say."

"Aye, most assuredly." Placing her hand in the crook of his arm, he leaned near. "We have been honored with another this night."

"King William has arrived?" Ailsa peered around her father, trying to get a glimpse of the great man. The hall was teeming with many people and though the thought of seeing the king appealed to Ailsa, she was searching for another.

"Nae," he replied. "'Tis the great druid Cathal. He

is speaking with Tam. Both will give the blessings this eve."

"This is wondrous, Father! If only he had arrived earlier for Tam to learn more from the elder."

He nodded in agreement. "As I was saying the same to Stephen."

"Let us proceed into the hall," suggested Aileen, taking her husband's arm.

As they entered the massive room, candlelight flickered against the stones, many adorned with greenery and tapestries. Several minstrels were playing a lively tune, and her feet tapped to the familiar melody.

Tables were laden with a variety of dishes—wild boar stuffed with mushrooms and onions, haddock in a dill sauce, quail filled with a savory chestnut and bread mixture, chickens crowned with eggs, a salad of dandelion and wild garlic, and an assortment of breads and tarts. Other dishes flowing with honeyed custards and sweets were set out on separate tables. Many of these tempting fares were ones she helped to prepare, and she could not help but feel a sense of pride in being a part of this celebration.

These were her people, too. Family. Though she ached for the people of Ailsa Creag, this was now her home as well.

Nell dashed over to her, holding a small kitten bundled in cloth within her arms. The young lass was forever finding animals in need of her tender care.

Slipping her hand free from her father, Ailsa bent down. "Ye have found a new friend? Was it lost?"

"Forsaken by her mother and left near the banks of the loch."

Ailsa gently touched the soft fur. "Or the mother

did not make it in this harsh weather."

Nell frowned in concentration. "Nae. She left to forage for food. Left the others behind. Sadly, I could not find them."

"This knowledge came from this wee one?"

Nell blinked. "Of course."

"Ye are a gifted lass *and* healer. Ye are welcome anytime on our island."

The girl looked away. "I thank ye, but I cannae leave my home here. Yet."

Ailsa placed a hand on the girl's cheek. "Nor would I want ye to venture out of this beautiful place. Only remember, ye have another place to call home, if ye so wish to visit."

"May I call ye Aunt Ailsa?"

"Aye, my lovely girl." Ailsa embraced Nell and then stood. Watching as the girl made her way to Brigid, she marveled at both.

Fiona and Deirdre waved to her, and she smiled in greeting. But her gaze continued to follow the flow of the hall in search of one man. She moved along the tables, nodding to several women or stopping to embrace the children as they scampered toward her in welcome. Her eyes darted everywhere for him, but Desmond remained elusive.

What if he wasn't coming tonight? The thought left her without breath, and she wanted to flee the festivities in search of him. Her nerves skittered as she steadily made her way past the crowd of people and out of the hall. The doors of the keep had been left open. Though the night was brisk, no threat of rain or snow threatened to invade. Her stomach roiled with uncertainty as she searched in vain.

A prickle of awareness skimmed across her skin. There in the shadows by the stairs, stood Desmond. Had he been watching her all this time? Her heart pounded as he emerged. Freshly shaven, he wore a dark blue tunic edged in the same silver pattern as her dress. The light from the torches danced off his eyes, illuminating the green within. The man drew her to him with his sweeping gaze, and her knees became weak.

"*Desmond*," she uttered his name in the hushed entrance.

Her hand sought his, and he brought her to his chest. "Ailsa, *ghrá*. Ye are a vision. A beauty which surpasses all others." Quickly glancing over her head, he pulled her back within the darkness of the alcove. Moonlight from the waxing moon spilled near the entrance by the doors, but they were safe from the light and prying eyes.

"I thought ye were not coming," she whispered.

"And miss the chance to be with ye on this last night?" Desmond lowered his head, and his lips sought hers.

It was a kiss for her tired soul, and she melted within his arms, surrendering to his touch. Soft bells echoed in the distance, and Desmond broke free.

"They are coming," he whispered against her ear.

"Who?" she asked, not caring if the entire world saw them.

"The druids. They herald the start of Midwinter. Will ye sit with me at the feasting table, Ailsa?"

She reached up and nibbled on his bottom lip. "Aye, and the night as well."

Letting out a groan, his mouth swooped down to capture hers again. The kiss left Ailsa with promises of more to follow. She intended on treasuring each moment with him.

Desmond stepped away from her. As he held out his hand his smile was inviting. "May I escort ye inside the hall, my lady?"

Lifting her chin, she complied. As he placed her hand in the crook of his arm, she looked up at his face. "Before we enter, I want to tell ye how fine ye look, Desmond."

His eyes darkened with emotion. She sensed he wanted to say something, but the arrival of the druids at the entrance halted any further conversation. Steering her quickly inside the Great Hall, he led her to the table where her father sat along with the other MacKays and their families.

Silence descended inside the place, and Angus stood. As the oldest Dragon Knight and Laird of Urquhart, it was his duty to welcome in the druids.

He spread his arms wide. "'Tis an honor to greet the druids who will give their blessing on this feast of light." While glancing around the room, his voice rang loud. "Urquhart has been blessed with abundance this year—in family, health, and crops. May we ask the Gods and Goddesses to continue to favor us with their love and protection." Turning his attention back toward the druids, Cathal and Tam, he added, "Greetings, wise ones. Ye are most welcome."

"'Tis an honor to be among the Dragon Knights and their friends and families," proclaimed Cathal. He motioned for Tam to move ahead of him.

Tam strode forward, holding a large log adorned with greenery. He bowed to everyone. "I bring the new to light with the old."

They both wandered slowly, chanting words in a musical lilt, their robes flowing softly.

When they reached the empty hearth, Cathal produced a small piece of kindling and held it up high. "Let us spark the light of Midwinter with the remains of the last Yule log." He waved it in the air and the bit of wood sparked into flames. The children gasped in awe and delight.

Tam set the new log on top of the other giant pieces of wood, and Cathal tossed the burning stick onto the log.

Both druids lifted their hands upward and raised their joined voices as one. "Let the lights from the stars cast their glow down upon the longest night which greets us once again. The land slumbers, and the battle between the Oak King and aging Holly King begins anew. Though the skies are cold and dreary, we rejoice in song and feasting as this night encloses us in her embrace. For we fear naught, since the moon and stars will light our path. Blessings of Mother Danu to all!"

Cathal scooped out a mixture of herbs from the leather pouch, belted at his side, and then tossed them into the flames. Sparks danced upward, and cries of approval echoed throughout the hall. Cheers resounded and many lifted their cups in salute to the blaze and each other.

Angus brought over two cups for the druids. "I thank ye both. Come and join us in feasting this night."

Taking the offered mug, Tam went and took a seat beside Bran. Lifting it toward Ailsa, he said, "Blessing to ye, lady."

Smiling, she bowed her head slightly to the druid. Taking a sip of her own mead, she savored the honeyed sweetness.

Cathal took a place next to Angus. "'Tis good to see ye once again, Desmond. Ye did not return with your brothers after Samhain?"

"'Tis good to see ye, as well." His mouth twitched in humor. "My sister considered it wise I should stay on until after Midwinter."

The druid cast a quick glance at Fiona. "A *wise* woman indeed." He turned toward Ailsa. "I am happy to meet ye, lady. I have heard your journey has been fraught with troubles. Thank the Gods ye came across the Dragon Knight and Desmond."

She bowed her head. "A great honor for us, Cathal that ye are here. And aye, we were fortunate to have the assistance of both men."

"How did ye manage to make the journey from Castle Creag? I thought ye were spending it with Cormac Murray and his wife," asked Desmond, reaching for a trencher of breads.

Cathal swirled the contents of his cup, before glancing at Duncan. "The weather was fine—no sign of rain or snow, so I left them in the care of another druid and sought the path to Urquhart." He tapped a finger to his head. "My sight told me I might be needed here."

"I am confused, MacKay," interrupted Muir, taking a seat near Finn.

Alastair leaned forward in his chair. "Which *MacKay* are ye referring to?"

"The Laird? Why would I speak of another?"

Angus arched a brow. "What has caused this bewilderment?"

Muir extended his arms outward. "Where is King William? Did ye not speak of him joining us for

Midwinter? Was it merely to impress us? Or did ye not deem us worthy to meet the man?"

Ailsa gasped and looked at her father.

Bran narrowed his eyes. "Why are ye showing disrespect to our hosts?"

"I merely asked a question," replied the man.

"I have already shared the knowledge with your chieftain as to why the king is not present," interjected Angus. "But since ye have not had a chance to speak with him, I will tell ye. The king is traveling onward to Arbroath Abbey to oversee the continuation of the building. We sent a messenger to tell him of the troubles with King John's men. We thought it best if he did not venture to Urquhart."

Filling his mug, Muir lifted it high. "I thank ye for *sharing* the knowledge." Draining the contents, he placed it on the table. Removing his dirk, he skewered a piece of meat from the boar.

Though the fire blazed hot, a cold tendril of uneasiness slipped within Ailsa at the silence around the table. Muir's behavior made no sense, and she could see anger in her father's eyes. Each day, the man attempted to battle the MacKays with words or blades. However, his manner with Desmond was far worse.

Angus waved a hand toward the minstrels, and they picked up their instruments. They filled the hall with a lively tune, breaking the tension at the table. He then took his wife's hand and led her away to start dancing. Smiling at the two, Ailsa filled her trencher with some of the tempting dishes in front of her.

"Did ye try the spiced apples?" murmured Desmond, placing several on her plate. "I am tempted to lap the juices from my fingers."

Her mouth went dry as she gazed into the man's eyes. Desire teased her within his emerald depths.

Ailsa finished her mead and attempted to eat some of her meal. He was correct. The apples were highly pleasing. Though the chicken and quail had become her favorite, it was the man next to her who she craved. Desmond's hand brushed against her fingers, and she stole a glance at him.

"Would ye care to honor me with a dance?" His smile was a moonbeam of promises yet to come.

"Aye, Desmond." Slipping her fingers into his, he tucked her hand into the crook of his arm and led her to where others were dancing.

They entered the circle and bowed to the dancers. The circle then expanded to include Desmond and Ailsa. Tapping her feet, she twirled and moved to the center with the other women. Grasping hands, they flowed with the melody, slowly and effortlessly until she broke free, and her steps led her back to Desmond. His hand brushed hers and they met in the middle, bowed, and circled the other. His eyes never left hers, drawing her into his web of only them. She danced around him, aching to touch him. The heat of his gaze stole her breath.

Onward they danced, twirling and swaying around the hall. Laughter filled Ailsa, along with Desmond's touch. As the minstrels ended their song, she dipped a curtsy to all.

Fiona handed her a cup of ale. "You were wonderful out there. I've never witnessed my brother dancing. He's good."

"Thank ye." Ailsa drained the cup, relishing the cool liquid.

Desmond returned holding two plum tarts in his hand. "By the Gods, these are delicious. Who made them?"

Fiona tried to snatch one from his hand. "Brigid. They're a favorite of Duncan's."

He shook his finger at her. "Nae. I brought one for Ailsa."

Fisting her hands on her hips, Fiona pouted. "But none for your *beloved* sister?"

"Ye wound me." Handing her one, he added, "Ailsa and I will just have to share this one."

Pleased with his gesture, Fiona kissed him on the cheek. Taking the offering, she was about to take a bite, when Alastair approached from behind her.

"'Tis good to see ye are eating." He placed his hands around her waist.

She laughed when he nibbled on her neck.

"Come, Desmond. Let us eat our fare away from the lovers," suggested Ailsa, tugging at his arm.

Snorting, he complied and followed her out of the hall and near the entrance. When he held the treat out to her, Ailsa took a bite.

Closing her eyes, she savored the sweet fruit and pastry. "Mmm…"

"'Tis good." He whispered softly.

Desmond's tongue teased the edges of her mouth, and snapping her eyes open, Ailsa yearned to have him kiss her.

"Go and announce to your father that ye are retiring for the night."

"'Tis too early," she argued in a low voice.

"Nae. He is most likely deep in his cups and enjoying himself."

She nodded and started to move forward when he grasped her hand. "I will follow ye within the hour." Kissing her wrist, he released her and leaned against the door, devouring the rest of the tart.

Licking her lips, Ailsa started forward and paused. She glanced over her shoulder. "And where am I to go?"

His smile became seductive. "To my chamber and into my bed."

Chapter Sixteen

"Wrap the kissing bough in twigs, greenery, ribbons, fruit, and wishes."

Desmond's steps hastened as he approached his chamber. His hand shook. He had waited nearly an hour before saying his farewells. His words to Ailsa were true. Her father was so deep in his cups that Angus and Duncan had to help him to his chamber, since Muir had left the feasting hours earlier.

Opening the door, he slipped inside the room. Candlelight flooded the chamber, bathing it in a soft glow. The flames from the hearth snapped, and warmth surrounded him. Yet, it was the vision sitting under the covers against the pillows that shone the brightest. Her golden hair shimmered, and his fingers itched to trail through its silkiness.

"Desmond." Her husky voice lured him to her. She leaned forward, the cover slipping free and exposing her luscious breasts. Her rosy nipples tempted him to come and feast.

The storm built within his blood to touch, kiss, and devour Ailsa. It clouded all other thought. Unable to speak, he stripped his tunic free and removed his boots. When he started to unfasten his trews, her hand covered his and stilled his movement.

"Let me."

"Ye are a brazen lass."

"Is it wrong?"

He shook his head. "Nae. I find it pleasing." Removing his hand, he placed her slender one over his swollen cock. "Set me free, Ailsa."

Her mouth parted and with trembling fingers, she slowly unlaced his trews, before pushing them down past his hips. Desmond gritted his teeth when she trailed one finger over the top and down the ridge of his shaft. He fought the temptation to push her back onto the furs and bury himself deep inside her body.

"Ye are magnificent. 'Tis hard and soft. I wish to do the same as ye have done to me." Ailsa moved out from the furs and knelt in front of him, mesmerized by his body.

Clenching his fists, he watched in a haze as her tongue darted out, teasing and tormenting him. Her hair fell over her face brushing against his thighs as she continued to explore his body with her mouth. His balls tightened, and he feared he'd spill his seed before he had a chance to touch her exquisite body. When she took him into her mouth, his vision blurred, and he let out a hiss. "Stop," he growled.

"Did I hurt ye?" Her voice was one of shock.

"Nae." He grasped her to his chest. "But my need is fierce and I cannae hold back."

She quirked a brow mischievously. "Ye have just arrived."

Desmond nuzzled the soft skin below her ear. "Yet, I have thought of naught else this entire day. My body has been hard and aching for ye."

"Then ease *our* torment, my love."

Cupping her head, he took her lips in a kiss that

was ravenous and unyielding. She moaned as he swept his tongue deep into her lush, warm mouth. He slid one hand down over her body, fondling her breasts and then sliding it lower until he came to her soft curls. Parting them, he trailed one finger over her sensitive core. Ailsa wrapped her arms around his neck, deepening the kiss. Hunger fueled their desire, each fighting for control. As Desmond continued to stroke the flame of desire, she whimpered and clutched at him.

Breaking free, she let out a cry. "Nae, dinnae stop."

He leaned over her. "I have only begun." Taking her mouth once again, he shoved them farther back on the bed. Her scent surrounded him, and his heart pounded in his ears. Desmond found he could deny her naught as he thrust deeply into her heat. Senses burning, emotions overtook him. Ones he could no longer shrug off, surfaced.

Desmond loved her. He longed to claim all of her—always. Not merely for this night, but also forever.

With a groan, he withdrew and entered her again. Bringing one of her legs over his waist, he thrust even deeper. "Ye are mine, Ailsa." Though he longed to tell her more, he found the words trapped within his heart.

She raked her teeth over his jaw, reveling in the sensation of him being inside her. There was no pain, only blinding pleasure. With each touch, stroke, and kiss, Desmond ignited a firestorm inside her body. Trying to match his rhythm, she found her own, letting it build. The tide of passion lifted her, and when he cupped her bottom, he widened the pleasure.

Higher and higher he took her, his breathing coming out in short gasps. Her lips sought his—hot and demanding. And then her body exploded into an array of bliss, lifting her high within the stars. Ailsa arched, screaming the name of the man who had stolen her heart.

Desmond's own guttural cry of release matched hers, and he shuddered violently in her arms.

Moments later, he rolled over onto his back, bringing her to his side. Her eyes fluttered open, and she found him gazing down at her. She swallowed. There was so much to say, and she didn't know where to begin.

Ailsa wanted his love, but dared not to ask for it. She wanted his heart, but feared he would break her own by refusing. She wanted him to stand with her on the ancient Stone of Claiming back in her homeland, yet dreaded asking him to give up his freedom.

Her lips trembled, and a lone tear slipped free. "I must—"

Desmond placed a finger on her lips. "Shh...*mo ghrá*. Come morn, ye can speak. For now, let me love ye. 'Tis all I ask of ye."

And as his lips sought hers once again, Ailsa reveled in his touch, letting him make love to her in places that left her senses reeling and begging for more. When sleep beckoned to both, they feared to waste a single moment and sat talking about their homelands. Ailsa watched Desmond's eyes light up as he spoke of his people and the land. Though he loved the sea, he found his love for the people even greater.

Curled up in his arms, she listened with rapt attention to him tell tales of his brothers. Their joy was complete when they were finally reunited with their sister Fiona several years ago. He'd explained the battle that had resulted in the death of their parents. They had summoned a Fenian Fae warrior to take their sister to safety, not fathoming she would be whisked away to a future time in Eire.

Between the husky burr of Desmond's voice and the heat from his body, Ailsa drifted off to sleep.

Early morning birdsong echoed within Ailsa's dreams. Her hand reached out, seeking the heat she craved. When she encountered naught, she blinked in confusion. Bolting upright, she brushed the hair from her face and glanced at her surroundings. For a brief moment, she pondered if last night was a dream, since she was now in her own chamber. However, her face heated, noting she wore naught under the covers, and her body waxed sore from all the pleasure Desmond had bestowed on her.

Her champion. Her warrior. Her lover. "Mine!" She shoved a fist against her mouth to stifle the cries.

Sadness weighed heavily on her heart and soul, and she tossed aside the covers. Cold air greeted her as she reached for a covering. As she walked slowly to the window, a lone tear slipped down her cheek. "How can I leave ye? Oh, Goddess, what am I to do?"

Biting her lower lip, she swallowed. Straightening her shoulders and lifting her chin, she moved away from the window.

****

Desmond rubbed at his eyes vigorously. Pacing within his chamber, he found himself torn. Taking Ailsa back to her room had ripped his heart to shreds. Honor had demanded him to return her to her own bed. Nevertheless, the man in him yearned to keep her safe within his arms.

But there was a fact he could no longer deny.

His mind betrayed him. Ailsa MacDuff was *not* his. She would return to her island and claim another for her husband.

Dark fury burst inside Desmond. Picking up a jug, he threw it across the room, the sound echoing within the cold chamber when it slammed against the stone wall and shattered.

"Nae!" His anguish cry pierced the room as he glanced in all directions. It was their haven for one night. Yet, he longed for more.

Grabbing his cloak, he stormed out of his chamber, vowing to never return. The room held secrets he would take to his grave.

Ignoring the shouts of Fiona and the other MacKay women behind him, he continued to stride with purpose. He wanted naught with anyone.

Steadily making his way along the corridor, his steps eventually led him to the stairs of the north tower. Flinging the door open, he let it crash against the wall. The blast of brittle air greeted Desmond and he welcomed its sting. The sky was bleak, and the hills empty and forlorn.

"Why?" he shouted into the wind. The Gods were cruel, he deemed.

He had been a fool. Love had entered his heart for the first time, and he longed to rip it free. His cloak slapped against his legs as he braced his hands on the rough stone. Misery and bitterness took hold of his soul, forever changing the man inside.

Never would there be another. Even the thought of returning to Navan left an empty ache within his chest.

Ragged clouds dotted the sky, their mists fingering

flimsy trails across a gray sky. He watched as a pair of hawks dove in unison, listening to their cries.

Desmond cast his gaze outward toward the trees, until his sight rested on the waters of the loch. There on the shore stood Ailsa and his heart froze. Alone. Her golden hair was unbound, whipping around her body, where only hours earlier he had cherished and loved the velvet softness of her skin.

He could not utter the words of farewell, even when he had placed her sleeping form on her bed. The thought of never seeing her again was akin to an arrow to the heart, and his breathing hitched. Bleak despair filled his soul while he continued to stare at her.

"Ye are a fool, O'Quinlan," uttered Alastair in a low voice.

Desmond clenched his jaw and ignored the man's intrusion.

"Her father is making ready to leave. They have released his wife's ashes in the water. Time is slipping away. Dinnae risk letting her go."

He glanced sharply at the man. "Leave me," he ordered.

Alastair shook his head. Moving away from the door, he approached Desmond. "*Dinnae* do what I did to Fiona. I ken those feelings of torment. They will continue to claw at ye. I once asked ye if ye loved anyone. If ye do so now, the pain of losing her will haunt ye forever."

"Bastard," growled Desmond and took a fist to the man's jaw. "How do ye ken how I feel? And I would never—"

The Dragon Knight staggered, but quickly recovered. Alastair rubbed a hand over his chin. His eyes blazed with his inner dragon, and his fists clenched.

Desmond fought to control his ragged breathing, and he wiped a hand over his forehead. Was that what he was doing? Letting Ailsa walk away from him? Or was he fleeing her? Did he fear her rejection if he uttered the words of love out loud to her? Could this be why he now stayed away? Never did he imagine love could shred a heart and soul to tormenting pieces. Nor bring him glorious joy. A double-edged blade, he mused.

He looked over the wall. His life stood on the shores by the white-capped water. And it all made sense. Turning, he faced Alastair. "Ye…" Desmond swallowed. "Ye were correct."

The Dragon Knight stepped forward and clamped a hand on his shoulder. "Good, since I dinnae want to take a fist to *your* face. Or worse, a blade."

Desmond smiled weakly. "Forgive me?"

Alastair sighed. "Aye. In love, there will always be battles. Now go to her."

Giving the man a curt nod, Desmond removed his cloak and handed it to Alastair. "'Tis easier to run."

Leaving the tower, he descended the stairs two at a time, and almost collided with Deirdre and Brigid at the bottom. Making a quick apology, he hastened out of the castle.

His heart pounding, he ran past the guards and through the portcullis. Dogs darted out of his way, barking at him as he sped past them. Joy and worry filled him the nearer he came to her, and his steps slowed.

Trying to calm his racing heart, he approached her

on shaky limbs. His mind raced with the words he wanted to convey, yet his tongue could barely utter one word. "*Ailsa.*"

Time stilled as she turned around to face him, tears streaming down her face. "Desmond," she uttered on a choked sob.

Striding toward her, he cupped her face and brushed away the tears with the pad of his thumb. His eyes roamed her features, and his breathing calmed. "I cannae let ye leave without speaking my heart. I love ye, Ailsa. I have naught to give ye *but* my love. My honor, strength, and body shall be yours. Will ye become my wife?"

He heard her indrawn breath and feared her reply.

She placed a hand on his chest. "Oh, Desmond, can ye stand beside me, knowing I will one day rule my people? Can ye give up your home—*your people*, which ye love fiercely? If so, there shall be no regrets years later. My heart could not bear ye slipping away from me with guilt."

His voice was hoarse as he spoke. "My *home* is with ye, Ailsa MacDuff. Your people will become mine." He wrapped his arms around her waist, cherishing the feel of her in his arms. "Ye already have my heart. Dinnae set me free to wander the land alone without ye. I have nae wish to become a hardened man."

"My champion. My *warrior*. Aye, Desmond, I will take ye as my husband and become your wife. Ye will stand with me on the Claiming Stone of my people. We shall both rule as one. I have *chosen* ye." She brushed a lock of hair from his face. "I love ye with all my heart."

Letting out a groan, Desmond captured her mouth,

sinking into the warmth of her lips. The kiss seeped through his veins, burning a path to his soul. Breaking free, he nuzzled her neck. "Can we marry right away?"

Ailsa leaned into him, brushing her cheek against his. "Aye, but ye do ken we must speak with my father." Nervous laughter bubbled forth. "He might want to take a blade to ye."

His expression turned somber, and Desmond pulled back. "I dinnae fear him. I will proudly walk into the lion's den and face the man. I *love* ye."

She laughed. "Kiss me again for courage and then we shall face the lion together."

****

"So this is where you are all hiding," pronounced Fiona, entering the north tower, along with Brigid, Deirdre, and Aileen.

All the Dragon Knights were leaning on the wall and gazing outward.

"We have a grand view of the loch," stated Alastair, drawing his wife to his side.

Deirdre handed her son, Alexander, to Angus. "What is so fascinating, husband?"

Brigid went into Duncan's embrace and looked outward. "Good grief! You're spying on Desmond and Ailsa?"

"Seriously, Stephen?" asked Aileen, reaching for his hand.

"We had to make sure Desmond offered her marriage," explained Alastair and placed a kiss on his wife's forehead.

Fiona poked him in the chest. "And what if my brother decided not to ask her? I thought you said this was *his* journey. Furthermore, what if Ailsa wants to leave?"

Alastair shrugged, but a smile tugged at his mouth. "I would have caused the ground to rumble, bringing forth boulders, and blocking her path."

Stephen wiped a hand across the back of his neck. "Or, I would have called forth the water from the loch, flooding the area."

Deirdre glared at her Dragon Knight. "You?"

Angus tucked his son close against his chest. "Surround the man and woman within a ring of fire until they came to their senses."

Brigid rolled her eyes and faced her husband. "Let me guess. You would have stirred up a massive snow storm, right?"

Duncan arched a brow. "I am nae that cruel. Only a fierce thunderstorm."

"Men," muttered Fiona. "Or should I say, *Dragon Knights.*"

All the women nodded in agreement.

Kissing her husband, Brigid started for the door. "Come on ladies. We have a wedding to plan."

Chapter Seventeen

"In the Highlands, one must always be on guard for a dark cloud among a sunlit sky."

Clasping her hands firmly together in front of her, Ailsa waited for her father to speak. His face was a mask of stone, matching the color of the stones in the Great Hall. Muir's stance was one of fury, but she cared not. She was not troubled by his lack of approval. Nae. There was only one she required. Fully prepared to do battle with her father, she tried to temper her impatience.

She swept her gaze to Desmond, noticing the tight strain of his jaw muscle, along with the hands firmly clenched behind his back. The moment he had stated his offer for Ailsa, the room became eerily quiet, and a sudden chill descended around all of them.

The flames snapped behind her father, mirroring everyone's mood, and she decided to take control. Taking a deep breath in, Ailsa released it slowly and stepped toward the man.

Relaxing her shoulders, she smiled and placed a hand on his arm. "I truly *love* Desmond. He is the warrior we need for our people. Did ye not take my mother from her own clan and bring her to the island?"

Bran's eyes softened. "She did not come willingly in the beginning."

"Truth? And here I thought ye charmed her right away with your flowery words of love," she teased.

His grin flashed briefly. Wagging a finger in front of her, he said, "Ye ken I am nae bard when it comes to words."

She tugged on his arm playfully. "I do recall Mother speaking of how ye would show off your skills in the lists. Ye tried to impress her with your strength. Although, she never did say what won her over."

Bran placed a hand over hers. "Aye, it did not gain her favor, and she called me a brute."

"What did?"

Her father cupped her chin and then glanced at Desmond. "I professed my undying love before departing for home. The next morn, I stood looking out from the ship toward Eire. I thought never to set my sight on the land again. My love was lost to me." Bran's smile broadened as he looked to Ailsa. "Yet, there she came, running down those rolling green hills and shouting my name."

Ailsa's eyes misted with unshed tears. "She loved ye as I love Desmond."

"Aye," he uttered in a hushed tone. Bringing her hand to his lips, he kissed her knuckles.

Turning toward Desmond, he gestured him forward. Reaching for the man's hand, Bran joined it with Ailsa's. "I grant your request to marry my daughter. Welcome."

"Nae, Bran!" shouted Muir in frustration. "He is an outsider!"

Her father moved toward the man. "My wife was an outsider. And ye have forgotten another truth. Your family was taken into our clan."

"But we have been loyal for generations," he argued.

Bran angled his head at the man. "And what makes ye believe Desmond O'Quinlan willnae?" He folded his arms over his chest. "If ye had your own desire to wed Ailsa, ye should have spoken sooner."

Muir's eyes darted around the room. "I have never stated thus."

Ailsa moved forward. "I have loved ye like a brother, Muir. Can ye not accept and trust my decision?"

He stared down at the floor. Several moments lapsed, and he finally met her gaze. "I wish ye well, Lady Ailsa." Giving her a curt nod, he strode out of the hall.

"*Muir*," she pleaded.

Desmond came to her side. "Let him be. He is a man torn."

Bran brushed a hand over his beard in thought. "Muir has been troubled ever since we arrived on Scottish soil."

Ailsa let out an exasperated sigh. "I reckon in time he will come to accept ye, Desmond."

He took her into his arms. "I pray so as well."

"'Tis time we celebrate this joyous announcement," shouted Alastair, entering the hall, along with his brothers and their wives.

Ailsa looked at Desmond. "How do they ken?"

Desmond narrowed his eyes at Alastair, though he fought the smile forming on his mouth. "I reckon the news traveled quickly after my words with a certain Dragon Knight."

Alastair gave them a wink as he presented a cup to

each of them. "About bloody time, too."

Desmond snorted. "Ye could have waited."

"Blame your sister," the man countered. "She was so overjoyed at seeing ye in each other's arms that she called forth the Fenian Warrior, Ronan—again—to stay your leaving." Holding up a jug, he added, "Now let us toast ye with our finest barrel of *uisge beatha*."

"What an honor," stated Bran, accepting a cup from Duncan.

As they all gathered around the couple, Alastair held up his cup. "May the Gods and Goddesses bless your union with love and happiness."

A rousing cheer resonated within the Great Hall.

****

The heat of the room, along with too much to drink and little food, left Ailsa feeling dizzy. Each time she looked at Desmond, her heart soared with love for the man. He stirred emotions she dreamed of, but feared never to find.

After informing Desmond she would return shortly, he brushed a soft kiss on her lips. Now, fresh air beckoned her, luring her swiftly outside the castle doors.

The entire hall teemed with every person at Urquhart—from the stable master, to the cook. They all had come to offer their good wishes on their forthcoming marriage. Though she tried to argue with the women on assisting with the wedding preparations, they utterly refused. Told her they would arrange everything.

Breathing in the crisp afternoon air soothed the dull ache behind her eyes. Her steps joyfully led her to the stables. Pushing open the doors, she went directly to

Elva.

"Greetings, lovely lady."

The horse snorted, and Ailsa patted her soft nose.

Pulling forth an apple from a side basket, she removed her *sgian dubh* from her side belt and cut a piece for the horse. Slicing one for herself, she chewed on the sweet fruit.

"Have ye heard the news?" she whispered in delight. She wiped away the juices from her mouth. "Desmond is returning with us. 'Tis a wonder this journey we have taken, my friend. I cannae tell ye—"

Sharp pain slammed into Ailsa's head. Fighting the inky blackness, she turned toward her attacker. Yet, the person was swifter and covered her head in a thick wrap before she had a chance to slash at them with her blade. Trying to fight whoever it was, she was rewarded with another blow to the head, and this time Ailsa faded into the bleak despair of emptiness.

****

A hawk's screech brought Ailsa out from her forced sleep. Blinking, she realized she was trussed up like a pig over a horse. Her arms were bound together, and a hood was placed over her head. The steady movement and her position made it difficult to stay focused.

Pain radiated down her neck, and the constant rocking motion of the horse made her ill. She blinked, trying to listen to her surroundings. However, all she could hear was the crunch of snow as they continued onward. Swallowing the bile that threatened to come forth, Ailsa attempted to calm her racing heart. Remembering her training, she tampered the fear, and brought forth the fury.

"I can ride, ye ken," she complained. "Bind me to the horse, if ye must."

Silence was her answer.

If the person continued on this path, she would surely empty what little she had in her stomach inside the hood. Resorting to another tactic, she moved, trying to free herself. "I am ill!"

The animal's steps slowed, bringing them to a stop.

Her captor shoved her onto the ground, and tugged at the bindings around her hood. As they came free, he yanked it over her head, and Ailsa took in huge gulps of clean, cold air.

"Ye should have all listened to me," snapped a familiar voice behind her.

Standing slowly and turning, Ailsa gazed into eyes that held hatred. A cold knot settled in her stomach. "*Muir*."

"Aye." His bitter stare raked over her body. "And remember I ken the way ye fight, so dinnae try anything."

"Explain," she ordered, trying to fight the wave of fury mixed with panic.

He sneered. "Dinnae command me in that tone." Pulling forth his dirk, he waved her over to the horse.

Ailsa tried to rein in her anger. "What are ye doing? Is this because of Desmond and me? Please tell me."

"The O'Quinlan bastard should have never come to your aid." Pointing the blade at her, he continued, "'Twas an easy plan. All but ye were supposed to die. For five long years, I have plotted, gained favor with those in league with King John, and finally an opportunity presented itself when your mother passed.

The lone requirement was Bran's death, so I would become the new chieftain with ye by my side."

Shock resonated within Ailsa. The man she had known her entire life had betrayed her family—her clan. When had he become a traitor? Did he fully reckon their people would accept him as their new leader? His mind was twisted. "*Why?*" Her question was laced with the hostility she could no longer contain.

Muir snarled and grabbed her braid, twisting it around his fist. He leveled the blade at her throat. "Because it should have all been mine ages ago. My family had claim to the isle, and it was snatched—*stolen* from my grandfather. Ye think we were taken in, but nae. A battle was fought and a choice was given. Accept the new chieftain or leave in dishonor. In the end, my grandfather relented. Yet, my father spoke of seeking revenge. Though he knew it would take time, he planted the seed within me. I plotted, *schemed,* for years. Kept it locked inside my mind. When my father died, I pledged a vow over his ashes that one day, Ailsa Creag would be mine, and the MacDuff clan would be squashed under my heel."

"Liar," she hissed, fighting the pain as his fist tightened more firmly.

Muir released his hold on her hair and punched her in the stomach. His laughter sent a chill down her spine as she fell to the ground. "How can ye rule when ye cannae hear the truth?"

Ailsa gasped for breath, even as her hands dug into the ground behind her. "I ken the story well, but it was your grandfather who started the rebellion. It was not his to claim. He became greedy."

"Now who's the one lying? Get up."

"Ye were our guard. *Our friend!*"

"I was *never* your friend. When we meet up with King John's men, I am handing ye over to them. By the time ye become King John's captive, I am sure your father will do anything to bring ye back, including forfeiting his own life. Ailsa Creag will come under English rule and since ye are now spoiled goods, I will take a bride. Perchance the English soldiers will find ye pleasing and take ye to their beds."

Standing, Ailsa faced her enemy. "My people will never accept English rule, nor ye as their chieftain. 'Tis mine."

He bristled, eyes narrowing. "Ye may think to be a warrior, but ye are simply a woman."

Ailsa's mouth tightened in disgust as he helped her mount the animal. *Your day of reckoning will come, Muir, and ye had better pray it is not at the end of my blade.*

The next hour was spent in silence while they climbed upward and farther away from Urquhart. The forest gave way to the loch below, and Ailsa studied the landscape, committing as much detail to memory as possible. If she escaped—*nae*, when she was free, she had to be certain of her direction. In her heart, she would not allow herself to be handed over to the English.

Muir might understand her fighting skill, but she had other ones, too. Deirdre MacKay had shared some valuable moves and insight to fighting. Considering the woman was a descendant from the great warrior woman, Scáthach, she absorbed as much knowledge from her as she could. Never did she reckon to need it now.

In addition, Ailsa knew the man's weakness. Aye, he was a strong and skilled fighter, but all the mighty could fall, including this man. He favored moving swiftly and at times, tired easily when angered. She risked her life in taunting him and stirring his ire. If the chance presented itself, Ailsa would have to fight Muir.

Shoving aside the mixed emotions, she now considered him her enemy. And her warrior mind turned inward at preparing a means of attack.

Chapter Eighteen

"The raven's cry heralded the arrival of the warrior, and the maiden scattered moonbeams to light his path toward her."

Uneasiness settled over Desmond. He blamed it on the absence of his beloved, but quickly shrugged it aside. Trying to keep up with the multiple conversations flowing around the table, he resorted to clipped sentences or nods. There was only one he wished to converse with, and she was not by his side.

Desmond drummed his fingers on the oak table. Deep in thought, he did not hear Alastair's comment, until the man was jabbing him in the side.

"Where are your thoughts?" Alastair leaned forward. "Where is your lady?"

Snapping his attention to the man, Desmond stood. "Forgive me. I shall return shortly."

Making long strides out of the hall, he glanced toward the stairs, thinking Ailsa had gone to her chamber. Quickly sweeping his gaze to the open front doors, he spied Finn near the well with one of the horses.

Walking over to the lad, he asked, "Have ye seen Ailsa strolling around the keep?"

Finn squinted thoughtfully. "Aye. She was heading toward the stables as I was leaving to take Gawain out for a ride. Perchance she required some peace with all the shouting going on inside."

Smirking at the lad, he made his way toward the stables. Upon entering, he looked around. "Ailsa?"

Hearing her horse, Elva, snorting heavily, Desmond raced quickly to her stall. The animal was pacing within, its eyes round with fear. Reaching out, he tried to calm the animal. Yet, his boot encountered an object on the ground. Glancing down, his heart froze. He knew the *sgian dubh* well. It was the one he had taken from his beloved when they first met. Never once did he ken her to be without the blade. Sweeping his gaze over the ground, he saw the discarded apple pieces and more. Evidence of a struggle was strewn across the stable grounds—from a half-eaten apple to baskets toppled over. Part of a sack had been emptied, its contents of straw dumped without regard.

His hands shook as he reached for a small piece of material snagged on a loose portion of the stall. He rubbed the soft bit between his fingers, recalling how he skimmed his hand over Ailsa's gown earlier in the hall.

Pure rage exploded inside Desmond, and he roared with its release. His beloved had most likely been taken by force and swiftly. His chest constricted with fear. Had the English invaded the walls of Urquhart? The mere thought of losing Ailsa slashed at his heart.

Finn was the first to reach him. "What is wrong?"

Desmond grasped his shoulders. "Prepare my horse. Ailsa has been taken."

"By the hounds! Aye! And mine as well. I will come with ye. I can track them."

"Agreed."

Storming from the stables, he rushed into the Great

Hall. "I require men to come with me. Ailsa has been taken."

Shouts and questions erupted within the hall, and Desmond held up his hands to halt any further words. "I found her blade on the ground and remnants of a skirmish are evident in the stables. Her horse is there, so I dinnae ken who has taken her."

"Have King John's men invaded Urquhart?" asked a stunned Bran.

"'Tis the bastard, Muir," snapped Finn, walking into the hall.

"Nae!" bellowed Bran, slamming his fist onto the table. "It cannae be!"

Finn shook his head. "His horse is gone and none of the other animals are missing. Even his satchel and sword are gone." Bracing his hands on his hips, he added, "If it was King John's men, why did they allow him to take all his belongings?"

"By the Gods, I will take his head!" shouted Bran.

Desmond snarled. "He was foolish to try and carry two bodies on one horse."

"Ye cannae be certain he's alone," argued Alastair.

"Will ye come with me?" Desmond asked the Dragon Knight.

"Aye, most definitely."

"As will I," proclaimed Duncan, coming alongside him.

Angus stood. "Stephen and I shall remain at Urquhart. With the threat of these men nearby, we will need added protection here."

Desmond nodded and turned toward Duncan. "I require Finn's aid, as well."

"What? No." Brigid came to her son's side. "I

won't allow him."

Finn glared briefly at his mother and then softened. He grasped her hands. "Ye cannae hold me back. I ken ye wish to keep me safe, but I am no longer a lad of ten. I have seen many a battle and 'tis time I learn to fight in them. Or assist."

Duncan approached and placed an arm around her shoulders. "He is correct, *my leannan*. Finn can track as well as any other. In fact, I reason him to be better."

Tears misted her eyes, and she bit her lip. "Keep him safe, Duncan."

Turning back toward Finn, she embraced him. "Come home to us and guard your father well."

Bran stepped forward. "I am coming with ye, so dinnae try and tell me otherwise."

"Your sword arm is of nae use, so can ye wield a blade with your left hand?" asked Desmond.

The man's smile was sinister. "Most definitely. The lesson was one taught by many on our island, though few could master the skill of using both arms."

Desmond placed a hand on the man's shoulder. "Good. However, I have one condition."

He eyed him skeptically. "Which is what?"

Desmond's lip snarled in disgust. "The Cameron is mine. Do ye understand my words?"

"Granted."

"We leave shortly. I shall fetch my sword and cloak." Desmond left the hall and mounted the stairs swiftly. Entering his chamber, he pulled forth his sword. Belting it to his waist, he withdrew a dirk from his trunk and placed Ailsa's *sgian dubh* inside his boot.

Going over to the window, Desmond bowed his head. Kneeling on one knee, he fisted his hand over his heart. "Guide us on our journey, Gods and Goddesses. Keep Ailsa safe from harm. Show us the path and give me strength. Ye have brought love into my life, I pray ye not to banish the light she has given to my heart and soul." When Desmond lifted his gaze to the gray clouds, a shaft of bright sunlight pierced through and hope surged within him.

Standing, he looked outward. "I am coming, Ailsa. Let my words carry to ye on the winds." Turning around, he strode quickly out of his chamber.

****

Squeezing her hands, Ailsa tried to bring some feeling into them. Her bindings were extremely tight, making it difficult to move her wrists. The rope bit into her skin, which was now raw and bleeding. Stretching her fingers, she continued to survey her surroundings. Anxiety clawed inside, scraping at her nerves. Surely Desmond would come searching for her. Perchance he did not ken she was missing. The thought wove a thread of fear inside her bones, but she banished it to the dark recesses of her mind. There was no time to consider uncertainties.

It was she against Muir. Time was swiftly becoming her enemy, and the higher they climbed, the more her chances of escaping were dwindling. It was unwise to attempt a fight with him on the horse. She had to put together another plan to remove herself. Only then would she be able to flee. If she could get away from Muir, she'd follow the loch toward Urquhart. Fighting him would prove foolish in her current situation.

A raven's caw pierced through Ailsa's thoughts, and she clenched her jaw. Was it an omen foretelling a doomed future for her? Squeezing her eyes shut, she sent out a prayer to Mother Danu, pleading for assistance.

I willnae die today. I dinnae believe ye would have opened my eyes and heart to love, simply to have it snatched away. Show me the light. Show me a way out of here.

"If ye reckon I am going meekly, Muir, ye have never known the true woman inside. Ye have become my enemy, and I shall fight ye to the end."

"Your words dinnae frighten me, woman."

"And ye are a loathsome, weak man." Ailsa clucked her tongue in disapproval. "I find it almost humorous to think ye see yourself as chieftain of our island. Ye must be daft in the head. The people would nae more accept ye than they would a young child."

When he yanked her braid back, his foul breath grazed across her cheek. "Do ye wish to die?"

Ailsa gritted her teeth against the pain. "And lose your chance at gaining favor with King John? I think not."

He pushed her away from him. "Beware your tongue, or I shall cut it out."

Realizing she was poking an angry boar, she trained all her senses on Muir. "Tainted goods will not be wise, either. Nevertheless, when I tell King John how ye schemed with the Dragon Knights to take over the throne…" Ailsa paused, hearing the low growl. "I have heard he favors beautiful women. Do ye really reckon he will believe your word over mine? I can be verra convincing." She half-turned and pouted her lips. "Would ye care for a demonstration?"

Fury exploded in his eyes, and he raised a hand to

strike. But as quickly as he did so, his face relaxed, and he cupped her chin harshly. "If ye think to taunt me with words, ye are more the fool than I thought. 'Tis a long journey we travel, and if I must bind your tongue, I will do so."

She eyed him scornfully. "Take your hand off me."

"Gladly," he replied.

Ailsa's head pounded in frustration, causing her heart to beat faster. She had to come up with a plan. Adjusting her position as best she could, she watched a lone wolf dart out in front of the horse. The horse whinnied and raised itself on its back legs. Taking quick advantage, she leaned with all her weight against Muir as he fought to maintain the reins on the horse.

"Hold!" he bellowed.

However, the animal continued to balk, fearing for its own life. In a desperate attempt to bring them all to the ground, Ailsa continued to lean backward with all her strength. Her actions proved successful, as Muir let go of the reins, bringing them both toppling to the ground. The horse took off at a fierce gallop through the trees.

Wincing from the impact, Ailsa swiftly rolled and stood. Not giving another thought to the man or animals, she fled into the trees. Muir's roar echoed all around, and her steps hastened. Fear drove her deeper into the forest. Without the use of her hands branches smacked her face, the sting of pain driving her onward. She would not stop. Not turn around. Not give up.

There was one light of hope shining a light on her path. Freedom and Urquhart.

Sunlight glittered through the canopy of trees as she continued to run. Jumping over a fallen log, Ailsa slipped and sucked in a breath. Pain tore into her foot, but she had no time to waste. Her arms ached, wanting to be free of their bindings, and her shoulders throbbed from the motion of being constrained. Birds flew out from the tree limbs, chirping angrily at being disturbed from their solitude.

When the crunch of leaves and grunts from Muir grew near, Ailsa went deeper into the trees. Picking up her pace, she darted as best she could between the trees. Yet, a sense of dread washed over her as the area unexpectedly opened to the loch below, and she slid to a halt.

Gasping for breath, she looked in both directions. One led down to the water, the other, along the ridge.

Turning toward her left, Ailsa bit her lip, undecided on which way to go, and finally descended the rocky terrain. Slipping several times, her injured foot screamed. Sealing off the pain, she cautiously crept along the narrow path. A cluster of pine trees loomed ahead, and Ailsa prayed she could reach them before Muir caught sight of her.

Her gown snagged on a fallen log, halting her progress. Tearing the material free, she continued downward. *Ye are almost there.* Rushing toward the trees, her fingers brushed aside the limbs, and she dove underneath.

Ailsa let out a long held breath and leaned against the rough bark. Recalling her training with Duncan, she closed her eyes and attempted to pull the mists around her. Cold and fear had her senses spinning in a tempest. Taking in deep cleansing breaths, she focused on the swirling tendrils of mists. Gathering the vision, she lifted her head upward. A light breeze kissed her cheeks, and she opened her eyes to find herself shrouded within the haze.

"I ken where ye are hiding, and ye will live to regret your actions." Muir's voice sent a strand of fear snaking down her spine.

Pushing away from the tree, she vowed the man would not put his hands on her again. "Ye bastard," she hissed into the cold air.

Instantly, a hand clamped around her mouth. Squirming against the intruder, she tried to butt his head with hers. Another hand slipped firmly around her waist.

"Stop fighting, *mo ghrá*. 'Tis Desmond." The warmth of his words spread throughout her body, freeing the tension. He released his hand from her mouth and turned her around.

She let out a hiss from the biting pain in her foot.

"Are ye hurt, Ailsa?"

"Twisted my foot," she muttered. Ailsa sagged against his chest. "Ye found me. 'Tis really ye?"

Desmond lifted her chin and took her mouth with a savage hunger. She drew his moan into her body and reveled in the strength of his touch. Breaking free, he wiped a lone tear that had escaped. "I would have searched the world for ye. But now, I must finish what the Cameron started."

Ailsa did not have time to utter a retort as Desmond sliced at her ropes, freeing her hands. He gave a short two-burst whistle and Duncan, Alastair, Finn, and her father emerged forth. "But—"

He placed a finger over her lips. "Dinnae argue," he ordered. His tone offered no room for argument, and she nodded. "Part the mists, so I may see him."

Closing her eyes, she steadied her breathing. Seeing the misty tendrils disappear within her mind, she slowly opened them to find Desmond staring at her. He brushed a gentle kiss along her brow.

"Be ready. He's charging down the path," muttered Alastair.

Gently leading Ailsa to her father, Desmond nodded to the older man. "Ye ken what must be done?"

"Aye," snarled Bran.

Ailsa clung to her father's arm. "How did ye find me?"

He pointed to Finn. "The lad is a fine warrior. Tracked ye and Muir's steps."

Reaching out for the lad, Ailsa embraced him. "Thank ye."

Stiffening briefly, Finn swallowed. "'Tis naught, my lady."

"'Tis *Ailsa*," she countered. "And ye are brave to venture forth with these other warriors. Ye are one among them. Did ye come upon the wolf?"

"Nae. Only the horse. 'Twas frightened, but unharmed."

Sweeping her gaze outward, she clutched a hand to her chest, watching as Desmond strode forth from the trees toward Muir with his sword held outward.

As the rest of the group emerged as well, Muir's steps faltered. Coming to a stop, his jaw tensed. He wiped the sweat from his brow, though his gaze never wavered from Desmond.

"What now, O'Quinlan?" he demanded.

Desmond leveled his sword at the man. "'Tis me ye shall fight, Cameron."

The man shrugged dismissively. "Ye expect me to

believe ye will fight fair?" He gestured at the Dragon Knights. "Will ye cower behind them?"

Desmond's eyes flashed with a thunderous rage Ailsa had never witnessed. His blade held steady as the sunlight glinted off the cold steel. "I have nae need for them. Your time of reckoning is here...with *me*. In the end, it shall be my blood on your blade, or yours on mine. It does not matter. This ends now."

Ailsa felt her father's fingers curl around her arm, and she darted a glance at him.

"Traitor," spat out Bran in disgust.

"And you're a thief! I should be the chieftain of Ailsa Creag. Ye have nae claim." Muir pounded his chest. "'Tis mine!"

Bran's chest heaved with fury. "Ye are dead to me."

"Enough!" shouted Desmond. Pointing a finger at the Dragon Knights, he ordered, "No one is to interfere. Do ye ken my words?"

Muir took the advantage of Desmond's momentary distraction and lunged toward him. Ailsa shoved a fist into her mouth to squelch her gasp as Desmond countered and blocked the oncoming attack.

The battle became brutal, as each man was intent on maiming the other. The clang of steel echoed throughout the serene setting. Though the two men were equally built, Muir had more muscle, and when Desmond slipped on the rocky incline, Ailsa once again kept her fear lodged deep within.

Blocking another blow, Muir swept low and slashed across Desmond's leg. A low growl escaped from him, and Desmond slammed a fist into the Cameron's face.

Blood spurted forth from Muir's nose and letting out a curse, he withdrew a dirk from behind his back.

"It will not matter how many blades ye show me, for ye are going to lose this battle!" shouted Desmond. Blood flowed out from his wound and seeped down his leg.

Muir's lips twisted in a cynical smile. "I will drench the ground with your blood."

As the fighting resumed, Ailsa could see Desmond weakening. Twice he staggered back, his injured leg now bleeding profusely. Her fingers itched to hold a blade and be by her lover's side. Her chest heaved with each blow, and the taste of blood filled her mouth from biting her own lip in worry.

When Muir slashed a blade against his arm, Desmond roared.

Ailsa's fingers dug into her father's cloak. "Ye—they must do something. I have nae wish to see Desmond die," she hissed out.

Her father shook his head solemnly. Gripping her hands firmly, his eyes were shards of steel. "Can ye not see what he is doing?"

Ailsa wanted to scream at her father. "I dinnae understand."

"He is proving himself to ye—to *our* people. If Desmond is to rule by your side, he must judge himself worthy to all. This is his test, Ailsa."

Her lip trembled. "Desmond has naught to prove to me. He is already a champion in my eyes."

"Yet, he must do so for himself. 'Tis his own honor at stake."

"So ye—the Dragon Knights would see him die?"

Her father tilted his head to the side. "Ye believe

he will, daughter?"

Fury boiled to the surface, wild and untamed. *Nae!* Her mind screamed. Wrenching free from her father, she reeled around. *Hear me, Desmond O'Quinlan. Ye will nae leave me all alone.* With her hands clenched by her sides, Ailsa lifted her head and prayed with all her might.

Yet, Desmond's strength faltered. He had managed to inflict some injury on Muir, but his wounds were worse. Deflecting another blow, he slipped and fell to the ground. Muir knocked his blade from his hand. Leveling his blade at his chest, he looked at Ailsa. "His life is mine."

Ailsa screamed. Stepping forward, her father immediately yanked her back against him.

Then again, Muir's proclamation was Desmond's advantage. Pulling forth Ailsa's *sgian dubh*, he knocked the sword away and shoved the blade into the man's thigh to the hilt. Dropping his sword, Muir collapsed onto the ground in agonizing pain.

Desmond stood slowly. Picking up the Cameron's sword, he flung it outward. Leaning over the man, he placed a booted foot on Muir's chest. Reaching for the *sgian dubh*, Desmond pulled it free and wiped the blood off on his tunic. "Ailsa's honor has been fought. Now, I leave ye to King William's men."

"And my champion has won!" shouted Ailsa, limping into his outstretched arms.

Desmond caught her with one arm, crushing her to his chest. Burying his face in her hair, he whispered, "*Mo ghrá*."

Tears spilled down her cheeks as she cupped his face. "Ye foolish man. Ye almost died."

He leaned his forehead against hers. "Nae. With ye my by side, I shall always win."

She felt her knees weaken as his mouth descended, sweeping her away with the healing warmth of his kiss.

Chapter Nineteen

Urquhart Castle, Early January 1209

"Two paths. Two souls. Two hearts. One love forged under a Highland Solstice moon, and the journey is now the beginning."

Warm sunlight danced over the loch, glittering like crystals. Geese flew gently overhead and Desmond watched their movement through the brilliant blue sky. The water lapped gently onward, the only sound in the area. Desmond breathed in deeply, enjoying the peacefulness and leaned against the giant oak tree.

Today he would be wedded to Ailsa, and joy infused his heart and soul.

Recalling the last few weeks, he rubbed his hand over the ache in his thigh. Upon returning to Urquhart, he found he could barely make it across the entrance. The wound to his leg so severe, complicated by the loss of blood, had weakened him enormously. It took two Dragon Knights to carry him to his chamber. Then another week before anyone would let him leave his bed. When he showed no signs of fever, they allowed him to take his meals by the hearth.

There was only one request before complying with their demands. He asked for Ailsa to take her evening meals with him in his chamber.

Desmond chuckled softly and brushed a hand over his chin in thought. The first evening, Bran escorted her and dined with them. On the second, Tam and Cathal entered with Ailsa. They proceeded to discuss numerous herbal remedies for sores, blisters, *and* the pox. Soon, he and his beloved found their appetite lacking, and the meal quickly ended. He let out a groan when on the third day, Fiona appeared with Hugh in her arms. For an hour, his sister babbled on about the babe's eating habits and fits of temper. At one time during the conversation, Ailsa paled when Fiona spoke of childbearing. Then the meal ended abruptly with Hugh wailing.

The fourth evening saw the other wives descend, along with their children. Not one morsel of food touched his lips during the meal. Each time he reached for bread, cheese, or a chicken leg, one of the children asked for a bite. Though he was smitten with them all, several considered it polite to sneeze, cough, or rub places on their bodies *before* reaching for a piece of his meal.

As the fifth night approached, Desmond found himself restless. All he wished for was time alone with his beloved. Yet, when his brothers, Niall and Brian walked into his chamber that evening, he could not have been happier to see them. Stunned, he found their sister had arranged for them to be magically brought to Urquhart for the wedding. The rest of the night was spent drinking, feasting, and talking until dawn.

Desmond would treasure that night forever. And so each evening afterward, Ailsa and her father dined with him and his brothers. Stories were shared, and a bond was formed between the O'Quinlan and MacDuff clans.

"Are ye sure this is what ye want?" Niall asked quietly coming alongside him. "Ye shall be missed in Navan. I ken ye love the lass, but to remain on the island, 'tis harsh."

Desmond folded his arms over his chest and smiled. "For the first time in many, many moons, I can say for certain this is what I want in life. Aye, I will miss ye and Brian—the people and our land. This is my path, and I love Ailsa fiercely. We will train warriors to not merely help the Fianna, but King William." He swept his gaze outward to the water. "My journey has led me to her."

"I am beginning to think our Fee is a seer. If not for her, ye would have returned home with us."

A chill brushed over Desmond, and he looked at his brother. "Truly. I must thank her."

Niall clamped a hand on his shoulder. "I am proud of ye. Will ye meet the Lion of Scotland?"

Desmond shrugged. "I dinnae fathom it will be anytime soon. When his men arrived with a message from the King, the letter stated he was riding south."

"And the Cameron?"

His voice hardened ruthlessly. "He went in chains with the men to Stirling."

"Do ye think it wise they leave him there? Does not King John control the castle?"

Arching a brow, Desmond laughed. "'Tis a battle still being fought. For now, I dinnae care what dungeon they place him in, only that he remains there."

Brian approached on the other side of Desmond, along with the Dragon Knights, wives, and family. Each embraced him with words of good cheer before stepping back.

Laughter pealed out from the gates of Urquhart, and Desmond lifted his gaze. His heart stilled, and he straightened. There Ailsa stood. Graced in beauty, her gown of ivory and gold glimmered in the sunlight with her hair trailing down around her in soft waves past her waist.

Desmond adored her. Never would he be parted from her again.

Watching as she strolled across the bridge and toward him, Desmond smiled. As her steps brought her nearer to him, his heart swelled. Their gazes locked, and she reached for his outstretched hand. Placing it on his chest, he whispered against her cheek, "Beauty beyond words, *mo ghrá*." She brushed a kiss over his lips, and he inhaled her sweetness.

Ailsa drew back and placed a hand on his cheek. "I have never seen ye more handsome," she uttered in a throaty whisper.

Tucking her hand in the crook of his arm, Desmond led her down to the water's edge. There would be two binding vows, one here at Urquhart and the other on Ailsa Creag. Cathal was chosen to oversee the one here, and Tam would do the blessing on the island.

Stepping forward, Cathal inclined his head slightly to them. "Though both your journeys were fraught with struggles, the path to love was greater. The Gods and Goddesses favor the union of the house of O'Quinlan and MacDuff. A stronger alliance will come from this joining."

Closing his eyes, Cathal lifted his arms upward. "We are gathered in this sacred place of old and new to be witnesses to the joining of Desmond Patrick

O'Quinlan and Ailsa Dara MacDuff." He nodded to Desmond as he pulled out the crimson cord.

Taking Ailsa's hand within his, he watched as the druid wove it around their joined hands and took a step back.

Desmond brought their hands to his chest. "All that I have is yours. Ye have already claimed my heart. I ken it was lost the moment I saw your face that cold morn." She laughed softly and he continued, "My world shifted, and ye took me inside yours. I will cherish ye always—protect ye with my life. When the storm clouds invade, I shall be there to bring the light and help ye push them away. I will love ye even when I take my last breath, for my soul is bound to yours."

Tears misted in Ailsa eyes, and she swallowed. Reaching for his free hand, she placed it over her heart. "I made a vow to marry only for love many moons ago and hear I stand professing all I have for ye. Ye are my home—the place I can find comfort *and* strength. Let our days be filled with love and laughter even when darkness surrounds us. My love for ye steals my breath and warms my soul each time I see ye. We are two souls, but will rule as one. My champion. My husband. My lover."

Desmond leaned near her, brushing his lips over her face. "Ailsa, *Ailsa*, ye are everything to me. From the rising of the moon to the setting of the sun. I am yours forever."

She choked back a sob. "Oh, how I love ye. Kiss me, my warrior."

His mouth covered hers hungrily, and he ached to be alone with the woman who held his heart. His arm wrapped around her waist, and he deepened the kiss.

Breaking free from their kiss, he noticed her eyes had darkened with desire. Leaning his forehead on hers, he whispered, "I long to strip the gown from your body and feel your skin under mine."

She teased her tongue along his chin. "Ye must be careful, since this is nae my gown."

He growled low and winked. "Dinnae fear. I can have another made."

Ailsa started to protest, and he silenced her with another soul-searing kiss.

A rousing cheer erupted from everyone, and Desmond broke free.

Cathal held up his hands to quiet the crowd. Smiling, he went over and placed his hands on their heads. Nodding to both Desmond and Ailsa, he proclaimed in a loud voice, "Let the binding vows be sealed forever, and may we ask the Fae to spread their light and love on your new path as one." Removing the crimson cord, he gestured his arm outward. "Blessings to Desmond and Ailsa O'Quinlan."

Once again, cheers broke out, and the glen resonated with warmth and love.

****

Desmond glanced at his wife leaning against the window in the Great Hall. Neither had slept and they both greeted the dawn after their wedding feast with a mix of happiness and sorrow. Ailsa had grown to love all at Urquhart, including his brothers. They had all fallen under her charm and deemed her worthy. It was a night they would not forget, especially when his brothers blocked their leaving to tell her one more story of his youth. He was sorely tempted to smash a few smiling faces, but they relented after she pleaded with them.

His brothers were smitten.

"Saying farewell is never easy," he uttered softly, placing his arms around her waist.

She leaned her head back against his chest. "Nae."

"Yet, I fear the conversation with Duncan and Brigid more."

"Do ye ken the lad is ready?" she asked, letting out a yawn.

"Aye. 'Tis time for Finn to venture out. His demons continue to haunt him. There are times when the past threatens to pull him down. Especially when he is around Nell *or* Brigid. He has shared some with me, but I reckon the past rears its ugly head in certain moments, reminding him of how he failed them."

Ailsa turned around. "But he was a boy of no more than ten winters. How could he have defended them all against a monster as Lachlan?"

"In his eyes, he saw himself as the protector—the man to challenge the evil. In the end, Lachlan sliced off one of his fingers and sent him back to Duncan with a message." Desmond searched her face. "Ye asked me if he is ready and 'tis a question I presented to the lad. I deem it wise to bring him with us."

Smiling weakly, Ailsa wrapped her arms around him. "A warrior at such a young age. We will train him well and embrace him as one of our own."

The doors to the Great Hall opened and Duncan, Brigid, Nell, and Finn walked inside.

"We had hoped to speak with only ye and Brigid," said Desmond uneasily.

"I requested to be present when ye spoke with them," stated Finn and gestured for everyone to sit.

Quirking a brow at the lad, he crossed his arms over his chest and took a seat.

Finn clasped his hands behind his back and took a stance, reminding Desmond of another—Duncan MacKay. Grasping Ailsa's hand under the table, he waited, noting the concerned looks on the lad's family.

Desmond inclined his head slightly toward Finn.

The lad lifted his chin. "In my conversations with Desmond, I find my journey is beyond the walls of Urquhart—"

Brigid gasped, and Duncan placed a comforting arm around her shoulders. "Continue," he urged.

"I am asking ye to give your blessing for me to travel to Ailsa Creag with Desmond. There, I shall train and learn the skills of the Fianna."

Duncan glanced sharply at Desmond. "I reckon you already ken this knowledge?"

"Aye. We have spoken, and I would be honored to take him under my care. Furthermore, he is a lad of thirteen winters. I believe the choice is his."

Brigid waved her hands about. "What is there that can be learned and not here?"

Finn's gaze never wavered. "I wish to one day travel with the Fianna. To help vanquish evil in other parts of the land. Father and my uncles might have destroyed the Dark One, but wickedness by others continues to spread. Is it so wrong to want to help others? To wipe out injustices for good? Tell me I am wrong, Mother."

Tears misted her eyes. "I cannot find fault in your decision, Finn. You have always been wise beyond your years." Standing, she went to him. "You do understand how deep my love is for you. I may not have birthed you into the world, but you are and always will be my son. I am proud of you. Yet, it does not lessen the hurt of your leaving."

Finn embraced her. "And ye are the only mother I ken."

Duncan placed an arm around Brigid and Finn. "Ye were a warrior that night I took ye into my care and now ye go forth to continue your training. I am proud of ye, as well."

Letting out a sigh of relief, Desmond's gaze shifted to Nell. Deep sorrow was etched across her face, and pain shone in her eyes as she stood rooted to the floor.

"Ye would leave our home? Ye would leave...*me*?" Her voice shook with raw emotion.

Finn stepped away from his parents and approached her. "Ye ken this is what I must do, Nell," he uttered softly.

"'Tis too soon," she whispered, while tears fell down her cheeks.

Smiling sadly, he brushed a lock of hair from her brow. "There would never have been a perfect time."

She swallowed and lifted her chin. "Then I shall say my farewells now, for my heart is broken, and I cannae bear to see ye leave."

"Forgive me, Nell." His voice and words were strained.

She wrapped her arms around his waist. "Be safe, Finn." Breaking free, Nell ran out of the room.

Lowering his head, Finn stared at the floor.

Brigid moved to her son and wrapped an arm across his shoulders. "Give her time. This is a shock for her." She glanced over her shoulder at Desmond. "I'll speak with Ronan when he arrives and request he bring you with Desmond and Ailsa next Samhain."

"A wonderful idea," stated Desmond and reached for Ailsa's hand.

Straightening from her embrace, Finn shook his head. "Nae. Perchance another time."

Frowning, Brigid simply nodded.

"I must make ready the horses. The Fenian Warrior is arriving soon."

Duncan stepped forward. "Let me help ye, son."

Finn smiled broadly. "Aye, Father."

Brigid retrieved Nell's wrap from the chair and hugged it to her chest. Her voice trembled as she spoke, "I do understand why Finn longs to leave Urquhart. Your island will bring him a sense of freedom. But no matter where he flees, the past will always torment him. He must confront, accept, and *forgive* himself." She turned her sight to Desmond and Ailsa. "All the training in the world cannot help him unless he releases this demon he carries within."

Desmond reached for her hand and placed a kiss along her knuckles. "I shall help him."

She wiped away her tears. "Sadly, there is no one to help him. Finn must travel this journey by himself. Watch over him and when the time comes to visit, please urge him to do so. Staying away from family is not a wise option."

Releasing her hand, Desmond watched her leave the hall. "What have I done?" he whispered hoarsely into the quiet room.

Ailsa stepped in front of him and wrapped her arms around his neck. "Ye did naught. I reckon the lad would have left his family at some point in time. An opportunity presented itself to him with ye, and I deem 'tis the right path for Finn. Dinnae let his haunts cause ye distress, my love."

Crushing her to his chest, Desmond held her firmly. "I fear the day when we have our own bairns."

Ailsa's laughter was warm, easing the tension from his body. "Oh, husband, let us not worry about bairns for now. *If* I am with child, we have another eight months to fret."

Desmond drew her back and his mouth opened in shock. "*Na...Nae!*"

This time, Ailsa roared with laughter.

Epilogue

The island of Ailsa Creag, February 1209

Standing on the cliff, Desmond watched the ocean waves roll and crash along the rocky shore. Inhaling the salty brine of the air, he glanced upward. Sea birds flew gracefully overhead, and he watched their flight. Closing his eyes, he let the sun's light warm his face and enjoyed the blissful solitude of the sky, sea, and land.

Upon arriving, they as well as the entire island were thrown into an upheaval of preparations for another wedding ceremony. Bran had called together all the high council members the day they had returned. He presented Desmond to those gathered and recounted the story of their meeting in detail—from the rescue of Ailsa to defending his daughter's honor by striking down the enemy, Muir. Even the story of Finn and his aid was accounted for inside the hall.

The Great Hall had erupted into a frenzy of shouts and banging of fists. All directed toward the Cameron. Shocked and outraged, they vowed to spread the news of the traitor. From there, Desmond and Finn were charged with greeting everyone on the island before the ceremony. For several days, they traveled with other warriors—sharing meals, and his and Finn's lineage. When they found out they were kin to the Dragon

Knights, they were instantly accepted.

Yet, Desmond's fears of acceptance truly banished the moment Ailsa took his hand as they both stepped on the polished Stone of Claiming near a cluster of yew, rowan, and pine trees. The druid, Tam, reported to him that Cuchulainn brought the sacred stone to the island as a gift to the people for their loyalty to the Fianna.

Therefore, on a crisp early morn, the entire clan of Ailsa Creag surrounded Desmond and his beloved as they once again recited their vows to each other. Desmond swore the ground shook and the air warmed afterward. But Ailsa assured him it was only his love for her and the people.

Desmond's heart and soul were now one with hers.

"So this is where ye are hiding, *husband*," chided Ailsa, her voice carried high on the breeze.

Glancing to his right, he smiled. Her hair had come undone from its braid, and she fought to control the loose strands as the wind continued to snatch them away. She walked steadily toward him, jumping over a boulder, and kicking away stones from her path.

His heart swelled. Ailsa was his sunlight and moonlight—warrior *and* wife. By the Gods how he loved her.

Opening his arms wide, he waited for her to step into his embrace. She snuggled against his chest. "Ye are so warm. I missed ye upon awakening. Dinnae tell me ye have grown weary of seeing my face."

Desmond lifted her chin up with his finger. "Never. I wished to greet the new dawn in solitude."

She arched a brow. "No regrets?"

He chuckled and trailed his tongue over her bottom lip. "Was not four times enough for ye last evening?"

She drew in a shaky breath. "Ye ken that is not my meaning. I meant—"

This time, he nuzzled her neck. "Aye, I do. And to answer your question…nae. Ye are my light, *mo ghrá*. I love ye with all my heart and soul."

Wrapping her arms around his neck, she searched his face. "I ken ye like to wander the hills. Do ye like the peace?"

"Aye, ye understand me well. This land is a beauty, and ye already ken my love for the sea. I will never tire of the view."

Her hands came down and she played with the strings on his tunic and splayed her fingers through the hair on his chest. "Good. Though, I do ken how demanding Father and my people can be. Ye shall be sharing stories of your adventures with the Dragon Knights and tales from your home in Navan until your dying days."

Desmond grimaced. "And now I have become a bard?"

Ailsa smacked playfully at him. "The stories are important to our people. Ye must give your account, so others will pass along the tales."

"Agreed. But for now, I have nae wish to speak about others."

"Are ye not overseeing the training for Finn? I thought to find ye in the lists."

His hands cupped her bottom. "Your father is with him this morn. I shall attend to him later."

Her tongue darted out, teasing Desmond and she pressed against him. "What is it ye wish to do then?"

Desmond's cock swelled in invitation, and he watched her eyes darken with longing. "Ye see that tree over yonder?"

"Aye." Her voice husky with desire. "Do ye have plans for doing more wicked things to my body?"

He nipped the soft skin below her ear. "What do ye crave, wife?"

Ailsa's face turned a rosy shade. "I find I can never get enough of ye."

Desmond rocked gently against her. "'Tis the same with me, *mo ghrá*. Let me love your body here. Feel the land, sun, and wind on our joined bodies."

"Oh, how I love ye, my husband, my *champion*."

Lifting her into his arms, Desmond captured her sigh with a passionate kiss, and the elements embraced the lovers.

A Note from the Author

I thoroughly enjoyed returning to Urquhart, the Dragon Knights, and finding a wife for Desmond O'Quinlan. In researching a name for Ailsa MacDuff, the path was a serendipitous find one afternoon. I saw a clear picture of her features within my mind, so I went through several names to fit her character. When I saw the Gaelic name of Ailsa, which means "fairy rock," I knew I had the perfect one for this lass. Yet it wasn't until I saw the mention of "Ailsa Craig," that my story was set in motion.

The island of Ailsa Craig does indeed exist. The island is approximately two hundred forty acres, which contains blue hone granite that was quarried to make hurling stones. It's located about ten miles off the southwestern coast of Scotland. Currently, the island is owned by the RSPB Nature Reserve and is home for Europe's biggest gannet colony and a significant number of puffins.

I've seen pictures of this island, and it's stunning. It was the perfect setting to place a fictional group of characters.

I do hope you've enjoyed Desmond and Ailsa's story. And have no fear, I'm sure to return to my own *Ailsa Creag* with future tales of life on this mystical island.

To read where the O'Quinlan brothers began, I encourage you to pick up a copy of *Dragon Knight's Axe,* Book 3 in the *Order of the Dragon Knights*. I knew then that Desmond, Niall, and Brian would each request their own story.

May your dreams be filled with Highland mists and Irish charm.

A word about the author...

Award-winning Scottish paranormal romance author Mary Morgan resides in Northern California with her own knight in shining armor. However, during her travels to Scotland, England, and Ireland she left a part of her soul in one of these countries and vows to return.

Mary's passion for books started at an early age along with an overactive imagination. She spent far too much time daydreaming and was told quite often to remove her head from the clouds. It wasn't until the closure of Borders Books, where Mary worked, that she found her true calling—writing romance. Now the worlds she created in her mind are coming to life within her stories.

Visit Mary's website, where you'll find links to all her books, blog, and pictures of her travels.

http://www.marymorganauthor.com

Thank you for purchasing
this publication of The Wild Rose Press, Inc.

If you enjoyed the story, we would appreciate your
letting others know by leaving a review.

For other wonderful stories,
please visit our on-line bookstore at
www.thewildrosepress.com.

For questions or more information
contact us at
info@thewildrosepress.com.

The Wild Rose Press, Inc.
www.thewildrosepress.com

Stay current with The Wild Rose Press, Inc.

Like us on Facebook

https://www.facebook.com/TheWildRosePress

And Follow us on Twitter
https://twitter.com/WildRosePress

CPSIA information can be obtained
at www.ICGtesting.com
Printed in the USA
BVHW041823081219
566035BV00017B/451/P